Stories by Contemporary Writers from Shanghai

GOODBYE, XU HU!

This book is edited and designed by the Editorial Committee of *Cultural China* series

Managing Directors: Wang Youbu, Xu Naiqing
Editorial Director: Wu Ying
Editor: Greg Tantala
Assistant Editor: Yao Feng

Text by Zhao Changtian
Translation by Yawtsong Lee

Interior and Cover Design: Wang Wei
Cover Image: Getty Images

ISBN: 978-1-60220-219-1

Address any comments about *Goodbye, Xu Hu!* to:

Better Link Press
99 Park Ave
New York, NY 10016
USA
or
Shanghai Press and Publishing Development Company
F 7 Donghu Road, Shanghai, China (200031)
Email: comments_betterlinkpress@hotmail.com

Printed in China by Shanghai Donnelley Printing Co. Ltd.

1 2 3 4 5 6 7 8 9 10

GOODBYE, XU HU!

By Zhao Changtian

Better Link Press

Preface

English readers will be presented with a set of 12 pocket books. These books contain outstanding novellas written by 12 writers from Shanghai over the past 30 years. Most of the writers were born in Shanghai from the late 1940's to the late 1950's. They started their literary careers during or after the 1980's. For various reasons, most of them lived and worked in the lowest social strata in other cities or in rural areas for much of their adult lives. As a result they saw much of the world and learned lessons from real life before finally returning to Shanghai. They embarked on their literary careers for various reasons, but most of them were simply passionate about writing. The writers are involved in a variety of occupations, including university professors, literary editors, leaders of literary institutions and professional writers. The diversity of topics covered in these novellas will lead readers to discover the different experiences and motivations of the authors. Readers will encounter a fascinating range of esthetic convictions as they analyze the authors' distinctive artistic skills and writing styles. Generally speaking, a realistic writing style dominates most of their literary works. The literary works they have elaborately created are a true reflection of drastic social changes, as well as differing perspectives towards urban life in Shanghai. Some works created by avant-garde writers have been selected in order to present a variety of styles. No matter what writing styles they adopt though, these writers have enjoyed a definite place, and exerted a positive influence, in Chinese literary circles over the past three decades.

Known as the "Paris of the Orient" around the world, Shanghai was already an international metropolis in the 1920's and 1930's. During that period, Shanghai was China's economic, cultural and literary center. A high number of famous Chinese writers lived, created and published their literary works in Shanghai, including, Lu Xun, Guo Moruo, Mao Dun and Ba Jin. Today, Shanghai has become a globalized metropolis. Writers who have pursued a literary career in the past 30 years are now faced with new challenges and opportunities. I am confident that some of them will produce other fine and influential literary works in the future. I want to make it clear that this set of pocket books does not include all representative Shanghai writers. When the time is ripe, we will introduce more representative writers to readers in the English-speaking world.

Wang Jiren
Series Editor

Contents

Goodbye, Xu Hu!

One

One winter afternoon, I sat in the café on the second floor of the Galaxy Hotel, looking out at a graceful little garden through a full length glass wall. The outside temperature had already dipped below zero; a cold spell had just descended on the city. However the lawn and the shrubs in the garden, bathed in the bright sunlight, retained a fresh greenness, giving a false impression that it must be as warm outside as inside.

I felt uncomfortably warm even after I took off my coat; the temperature in the hotel was set too high for local Chinese preferences. I wished I could bag the excess heat and take it home in a doggy bag.

I was waiting for a friend who had

returned from abroad; I was a little early and was nursing my coffee, killing time sip by sip and watching the people walking into the lobby. Then I saw Xu Hu. I did a double take and involuntarily got to my feet. Was it really Xu Hu? Yes, it was! Time seemed to have treated her with a special leniency and kindness; she retained her finely proportioned, slender figure and her delicate, pretty facial features. Only, her beauty was now enhanced by the charm of a mature woman. I opened my mouth to call out to her but failed to produce a sound.

My awkwardness caused several guests enjoying their coffee to look up at me. She also cast a glance in my direction, without recognizing me, and went to a table in a corner by the window. As she sat down, she took another look over her shoulder at me. I sat down quickly, but kept my eyes focused on her.

The café was not crowded and as the three tables separating us were all unoccupied I had a clear view of her. I observed her with outward calm, but emotions churned in my chest. My heart beat wildly. I felt like walking up to her and asking, "May I sit down?" If she still didn't recognize me, I would say, "Don't you recognize me? I am ..." But I didn't move from my chair. I wondered why she didn't show any sign of recognition. Could I have mistaken a stranger for her? All of a sudden I wasn't so sure of myself and found myself feeling somewhat absurd. What made me so certain that she was Xu Hu? There are many doppelgangers in the world after all. With this thought, I relaxed and took a few sips of coffee, trying in the meantime to conjure up what she looked like in her youthful years. Strangely enough, I couldn't recollect what she looked like when she was young. Try as I might I could not form a clear, distinct picture of her!

I had always regretted not keeping a photograph of Xu Hu. Because of the haste and abruptness of our breakup, I never had the chance to ask her for one. She had been living in my memory all these twenty years and yet I was now unable to determine which bits of my memory of her were true and which were merely figments of my imagination caused by the painful years of longing for her. Figments of imagination about her were no doubt included in my memory, in which beautification usually took the major part.

I studied this woman. She was dressed elegantly and with care; her makeup was done with fine taste and was very becoming. Everything about this woman bespoke social status and wealth. As I watched her, she became more and more like a stranger to me, and farther from the Xu Hu in my memory. But I couldn't take my eyes off her. The sight of her rekindled a longing for Xu Hu. What had become of Xu Hu? I wondered.

She beckoned the waiter over and ordered a drink, casting another glance in my direction. Maybe she had become aware of my constant staring. Realizing my rudeness, I quickly turned my head to look out the window. All of a sudden she pushed her chair back and stood up, creating a loud noise due to the abruptness of her movements. I immediately guessed she'd finally recognized me and that she was indeed Xu Hu.

"You are ..." she asked as she came up to me.

"Yes, I am Zhou Shuting." I pulled a chair for her.

She remained standing and asked in startled joy, "Are you really Zhou Shuting? Didn't you recognize me the minute you saw me?"

I nodded.

"How did you recognize me immediately? I've aged a lot."

"You haven't. You are still as pretty as ever."

She laughed, "Since when have you

learned how to flirt?"

I shook my head, "No, it was not flirting. You are pretty and I think you know it."

"But I am already 38 ... I still can't get over the fact that you were able to spot me so quickly when we bumped into each other under such unexpected circumstances."

"Put it to telepathy," I quipped.

Maybe telepathy was the only explanation. It all happened, after all, 20 years ago, when she was an 18-year-old girl in a plain military uniform, still showing residual traces of her childlike manners ...

TWO

It was the pair of shoes Xu Hu was wearing that first attracted her to me.

Xu Hu was admitted, after successfully passing a test, to our wen gong tuan, a cultural troupe undertaking tours to entertain troops, when she was almost 17 years old. In the wen gong tuan, famed for the beauty of its female performers, Xu Hu did not particularly stand out for her good looks. At the time I had recently been transferred, from a rank-and-file position to the political department of the military as a creative writer. My job description included writing pieces to be performed by the cultural troupe. Although I was organizationally part of the cultural service, I was assigned a room in the dormitory compound of the cultural troupe. The dormitory compound, located in a place called Sanshi village in the southern outskirts of Chengdu, consisted of a few one-story buildings set around a concrete basketball court. I lived in a suite with the inner room as my bedroom and the outer room serving as the office of the creative writing team. It so happened that two of the three creative writers had homes in Chengdu and did not have to come to the office every day as they could write at home; this allowed me to use the office as my personal study. I would sit by the window reading and writing to my heart's content. When tired, I could look up from my work through the branches of the magnolia and pomegranate trees in front of the porch, and watch the troupe members practicing on the basketball court. Rachmaninoff's Italian Polka played while troupe members rose up on the tips of their toes and back down, up again and down again, repeatedly, to the beat of "1234, 2234 ..." belted out by the dance teacher from the cultural troupe of the political division of the Air Force. Even now, after so many years, whenever this Italian Polka is played, a mental picture of a group of young women practicing their dance steps is conjured up and I think of how blessed I was to be able to feast my eyes on those beautiful young women. But, surprisingly, when I had the good fortune to see those pretty girls parade before my eyes day in and day out, I seemed to have hardly paid any heed to them.

Of course it is not true that I hardly paid any heed to them. I was physiologically and psychologically normal after all. But that was an era when you were supposed to keep your desires in check. In a strictly puritanical environment, the slightest "temptation" could lead to forbidden fantasizing. In that day and age, fantasizing about the opposite sex remained mostly in the realm of dream and imagination, not least because I was under strict military discipline.

I was then 27, and did not have a marriage prospect. I had a girlfriend before, a girl who went to the same high school and who kept up correspondence with me after I entered the military. Somehow this relationship was discovered by the political instructor of my military unit, who called me in for a "talk." The girl and I never declared our love in our letters, which were devoid of intimate, romantic language. In fact our letters were so inspired by "revolutionary zeal" they would have been perfect as party propaganda. But I admitted to the instructor that she and I liked each other and that the correspondence may result in marriage. "Soldiers are forbidden to maintain romantic relationships," the political instructor told me with a stern expression. I did not put up any defense in reply. I accepted the order without a word of protest and put an immediate halt to my correspondence with her. A year later

I was promoted to platoon leader. The day after the announcement of my promotion, the political instructor had another talk with me. This time he said I could now give thought to my "personal business," a euphemism for marriage prospect, as if by merely thinking about it I could find an instant fix for this "personal business."

You would think that given the daily exposure to so many pretty girls in the cultural troupe, I had an excellent opportunity to take care of my "personal business." But like many Shanghainese in the military, I wanted a Shanghai girl for my wife. Besides, the performers of the troupe were soldiers and consequently forbidden by military policy to get romantically involved too. I had no desire to get them in trouble.

One day, for some obscure reason and certainly not by design, I noticed the shoes Xu Hu was wearing. In that era the performers of the troupe were plainly dressed. They normally wore military-issued "Liberation" shoes or black-faced white-sole cloth shoes with an elastic band across the top. But Xu Hu wore a pair of men's round-cut cloth shoes with two cloth strings tied around each ankle, looking much cruder than the military-issued cloth shoes with elastic uppers. She wore those shoes for her practice sessions and instead of taking them off after practice she wore them everywhere. It was my guess that her shoes were the handiwork of the peasants among whom she had sent to be "reeducated" during the Cultural Revolution. I was favorably impressed by the fact that she felt comfortable in those unsophisticated peasant shoes.

One day the band conductor walked in when I was watching the troupe in practice. I asked, pointing her out, "What's her name?"

"Xu Gao."

I asked him how the character "gao" was

written in Chinese. He told me. But when I looked it up in the dictionary later, I found out it should be pronounced "hu" and denoted a swan, although the same character had a second pronunciation "gu" which would mean an archery target. According to the explanation of the dictionary, the first pronunciation should be adopted in her name. Many in the cultural troupe, however, had mistakenly pronounced her name "gao."

"She comes from a high official's family," added the band conductor.

"Really? She doesn't look it. She appears so unpretentious. What does her father do?"

"I don't know."

I didn't pry further. After all it was just an idle question. Although I was favorably impressed by her, it was nothing more than that and I had no plans for deeper involvement with her.

During this time, I finished writing

a one-act play entitled The Mountain Is High and the River Is Long, a story about the friendship and solidarity between an educated young woman sent to the countryside and an old man from a military family. The theme of the play was the "hand and glove" relationship between the military and the people. During casting, Xu Hu immediately sprang to mind. I wanted her to play the lead female role. I mentioned her cloth shoes as proof that she empathized with the poor peasants. My choice was quickly approved. I found that the leadership of the cultural troupe were impressed by her too.

Normally once the script was approved, rehearsal had nothing to do with me. If I wanted I could watch from the sidelines, but it would be perfectly all right if I didn't. Lao Du, the director of the troupe, happened to have been seconded to the cultural troupe of the military region, so Lao Ding was now not only playing the old man in the play, but also the role of acting director. Lao Ding was good with body language but was in over his head with character analysis. He did a passable job of understanding his own role but when it came to treating the inner logic, the dynamics of the interactions of characters or directing Xu Hu's interpretation of her role, he fell short. So the troupe leader came to me for help.

So it came to pass that I was with Xu Hu nearly every day of the month-long rehearsal.

March was the best season in Chengdu. There was rarely any sun in Chengdu in the winter; it was usually cold and damp. When spring came, the sun suddenly made a comeback and the dark moods that festered all winter evaporated under the sun and my heart bloomed with joy. The wonderful thing about spring in Chengdu was that it rained nearly every evening but shone invariably during the day. The all-night drizzle washed away all the filth in the air and gave a new sheen to the leaves and flowers in the city. When one opened the window in the morning and looked out on the glittering puddles on the road surface, one could not help but feel exhilaration.

The compound of the cultural troupe was situated by the beltway that surrounded the city. Across the highway was a large oilseed rape field, which became a vast carpet extending to the horizon in March, when the rape plants bloomed. In the late afternoon we would stroll in groups of three or four on the shoulders of the highway or on the ridges dividing the field into parcels, and return to the compound only when it was dark. After taking the job of "assistant director," I had many such walks accompanied by Xu Hu. It was naturally a pleasant task to enjoy those evening promenades with a pretty, young girl and I was not one to turn down such opportunities when there was a perfectly legitimate excuse, at least initially, of discussing the script and characters with her. When we became better acquainted following a period of shop talk, our conversations became less inhibited and I eventually asked her, "Do you know why you were asked to play this character?"

"I know."

"You know?" I was surprised. "How did you know?"

"Didn't you recommend me for the role?"

"Oh," I said, "That's not what I meant. What I asked was why you. Why you were recommended for the part and not someone else."

"I don't know. Why?" she stopped and looked at me queryingly.

"Because of your shoes."

She happened to be wearing those blunt-nosed masculine shoes. Her face became flushed when she sensed my glance at her feet and she shifted one foot behind the other as if trying to hide both.

"Were they made by peasant folks

in the place where you were sent to be reeducated?"

"Oh, no."

"Then who made them?"

"My maternal grandmother."

"Your maternal grandmother … lived in the countryside?"

"In Shandong Province."

"Is your family originally from Shandong?"

"Yes, but I was born in Zhejiang Province."

We started talking about our respective families. I learned that her father was in the military, and she had accompanied him since childhood on his tours of duty across China, her longest stay being in a fortification in Zhoushan in Zhejiang Province. I was surprised to learn she could speak the Ningbo dialect! I was surprised and instantly felt closer to her because Ningbo happened to be my ancestral town. A thought flashed across my mind, I could have her as my wife … but no sooner had the thought entered my consciousness than my cheeks burned with shame. Wouldn't that leave the impression that the whole thing, including my recommendation of her for the part, was a carefully premeditated plan? Besides, she was barely 18 at the time, so my thoughts became automatically moot under both military regulations and marriage law. But laws and regulations are not lethal enough to kill thoughts. Many thoughts can be no more ignored than babies after they have been conceived and given birth to. Those thoughts, tinged with desire, grow wings and the more you try to keep them grounded the higher they will soar.

When the rehearsal stage was over and the play was ready for the stage, we lost the excuse for our walks through the oilseed rape field. Our conversations, truth be told, had long strayed away from the play. Precisely for that reason the desire for continuing these walks and having conversations unrelated to the play became stronger.

That night we strolled longer than usual. We lingered in the field even after it had become pitch black. The rape flowers had wilted but a residual fragrance rose from the soil. We began to walk back slowly; shortly before reaching the highway we simultaneously came to a halt, as if it had been planned. I felt Xu Hu's body gently, softly leaning into mine when she whispered that she was fond of me. It was a soft whisper but I heard it. I would have heard it even if her voice had been lower, because she said what I also wanted to say to her. I took her gently into my arms, gingerly, and with trepidation as if a greater force would break this delicate, treasured piece of china. But I could feel her body tightly pressed against mine.

Three

I snapped out of my reverie and remembered Xu Hu was sitting there, waiting. "What would you like to have?" I asked.

She responded with a question. "Are you waiting for someone?"

"Yes."

"Who is it?"

"A friend who's visiting from abroad."

"Someone very important to you?"

"Not really."

"Not as important as I?"

I laughed, "Certainly not."

"Then let's leave." Getting to her feet, she said to the waitress, "If someone asks for a Mr. Zhou, please tell him that Mr. Zhou was called away on urgent business and will get in touch with him later. Oh, yes, never mind the coffee I ordered. Here, this will settle the check."

I cast another glance out the full length window, my mood now as bright as the sunlight outside.

In the elevator I asked, "What were you here for?"

She said with a smile, "I had several things to attend to, but now only one thing remains to be done."

"And that is?"

"Talking with you."

She was staying in a well-appointed standard room on the 17th floor of the Galaxy Hotel. After hanging a "Do Not Disturb" sign on the outside door knob and closing the door, she took her cell phone from her purse and turned it off and then asked the hotel operator to block all incoming calls. After taking care of those details, she took a bottle of red wine from the refrigerator. As she poured the wine she said, "Now that we will be undisturbed, we can talk in quiet privacy."

It was indeed very quiet, but I didn't know what to say. I was still replaying in my mind all her movements up to that moment, without missing a single detail. My eyes had not left her since she came into my view that day. I couldn't help it. After all we had lost touch for twenty years and I had been thinking about her for that whole time. How could I afford to waste this opportunity of locking her in my sight when this woman who had haunted my thoughts and my dreams for twenty years had miraculously materialized before my eyes?

But what could I say? It was twenty years, not twenty days, of separation. Twenty years was almost a lifetime. In the initial excitement of our chance meeting, I entertained an illusion that we could revive our past romance and fond memories by simply wishing away the intervening years. An illusion fueled by her high spirits and young appearance. That was ridiculous of me. How could a forty-something still be so naïve! I was so ashamed of myself. Look at her! How she breezed through the preparative steps leading up to the private rendezvous! Such self-assurance and skillfulness! I wondered how many men she had had in her life; she exhibited such sophistication in dealing with men. I congratulated myself for cooling down before our conversation began in earnest, before I made a fool of myself.

I commented, "You went through the whole routine so effortlessly."

She said with a laugh and a sigh, "I have to. It's always one thing or another that I have to deal with day in day out. People come to me for every tiny thing. If you don't master the art of an escape artist, you won't be able to accomplish anything."

"Are you in business?"

She nodded.

"Doing well?"

"I'm surviving. What about you, what do you do?"

"Editing for a magazine."

"Chief Editor?"

"No, director of the editorial board."

"Don't you write for yourself?"

"I scribble for some extra income."

"How's your family? What does your wife do?"

I shook my head.

She stared at me in disbelief. "You don't have a wife? You are not married?"

"I was," I said, "but now I'm divorced."

"Why?"

"What else? Incompatibility, loss of mutual affection, stuff like that."

"I don't want to hear the boilerplate language used in divorce documents."

I fell silent.

"Why have you never tried to contact me?"

I remained silent.

"Have you ever thought about contacting

me?"

"Yes."

"Then why didn't you?"

"You should know … besides you have never contacted me either."

"Sorry. I did not mean to bring up unpleasant memories for you, I merely … all right, I'll stop here."

"Yes, let's not talk about it. Let's talk about the happy moments we shared."

Four

In a collective environment, it was impossible to keep intimate relationships secret. I was fully prepared to face and accept the harsh criticism from our leadership and even disciplinary action. But none came. In fact, when we thought we were safely covered by the pretext of discussing the rehearsal, everybody, including the leadership, already saw through the subterfuge, but they had adopted a surprisingly lenient attitude concerning the matter. Initially I attributed the leniency partly to the fact that I was not on the regular staff of the cultural troupe and believed that they looked the other way because my job performance was well regarded and I generally maintained a good rapport with everybody. When I discussed these thoughts with her, she merely said with a laugh, "It's possible."

We were no longer underground lovers but could now openly meet. We were lucky in that I mostly had a suite to myself so that we could be together without being disturbed. But in reality our relationship consisted merely of talking even when we were alone together and the bulk of time was spent on pursuing our respective reading interests. Some of the books in the collection of the creative writing team were purchased, with written consent issued by the political department, from a restricted-access bookstore. They were mainly pre-Cultural Revolution magazines and Soviet novels, such as Kochetov's The Secretary of the Obkom and Ivan Shamiakin's Snowy Winters, published for the sole reading pleasure of the party cadres. These books are now read by few but were much prized in those days. Sometimes I recounted to her stories from novels I read before entering military service. I had told these stories to my comrades in the company guarding a radar station in a remote mountain isolated from the rest of the world. The culturally starved comrades in arms mined all the stories in my head. Some of the most well received ones were repeatedly retold as showpieces and I could reel them off with ease. The art of my storytelling was honed to an exalted level and all the more colorful and graphic because I was telling the stories to a girl I desired. Xu Hu was an ideal listener; she was quick to grasp the gist of the story, and her emotion followed the ups and downs and twists and turns of the story so that my storytelling always struck the right chord with her. She had a hearty, uninhibited laugh, simple and straightforward, which was very endearing. The yearning to show off my storytelling talents found in her an ideal vent. Storytelling was also a perfect excuse to look fixedly and boldly into her big, beautiful and expressive eyes. The admiration for my talents, evident in her eyes, sweetened me to my soul, sweeter than honey. At such moments I had a strong impulse to take her in my arms, caress her, kiss her, and even … but I did not have the courage. I was afraid that a rash move would ruin her perception of me. It's not that I had never held her in my arms before, but it was under cover of night and in a deserted field. Besides it happened spontaneously, almost subconsciously. In a well-lit room, face to face with her, I could not bring myself to spontaneously and self-assuredly take her into my arms. My boldest move was to take her delicate hands into mine at climactic or suspenseful moments in the story. In this day and age, hand holding between girls and boys has become quite casual and commonplace, but in those days, it was an intense form of romantic expression. The first time I held her hand, I could feel it trembling and was so electrified by the touch that I couldn't continue with the story. We just held each other's hands, looking into each other's eyes without uttering a sound, until our hands were drenched in sweat.

After a few more such instances of handholding, Xu Hu invited me to her home. It was a Saturday evening. After I finished telling the story of "The Gift of the Magi," a short story by O. Henry, she was silent for a long spell, relishing the clever story line and overwhelmed by the noble, genuine sentiments of the protagonists. This time she took the initiative and reached out and put her hand on mine, gently rubbing it. She then said, "Shuting, if I invite you to my home, will you go?"

"When?" I asked.

"Tomorrow," she said after considering it.

I nodded. Realizing the significance of the invitation for our relationship, I was overjoyed. For the occasion I changed into a military uniform that had been worn only once. This uniform had a brand new crispness about it and was properly ironed and creased and fit me perfectly. I sneaked into the rehearsal hall to look at myself in the big mirror; I quite admired my smart looks.

The next morning, we left the compound separately and regrouped outside the Temple of Marquis Wu (a shrine to Zhuge Liang, the prime minister of the Shu dynasty), from there we took a bus to the headquarters of the greater military. I had never been to the greater military headquarters before. The Eighth Corps of the Air Force was under the direct jurisdiction of the Beijing military commission. Administratively our creative writing team was supervised by the cultural division of the political department of the Air Force and professionally had no dealings with the air command of the military.

I paused before the archway at the entrance of the complex. Xu Hu urged me to go in. I tried to appear relaxed and gave a casual but standard military salute when I passed the sentinel box. The sentry at the gate immediately responded with a "present arms" salute.

Xu Hu commented with a laugh, "That was a smart salute."

"Don't forget I'm a seasoned soldier," I said.

The compound was huge. Xu Hu showed me around, pointing out the buildings that housed the command center, the political department, the officers' club, and the PX. As we went deeper into the compound, we came to another compound, enclosed within the compound. This one was densely planted with trees and guarded by another sentry. I followed Xu Hu as she prepared to enter the compound within the compound. The sentry snapped to attention and called out, courteously but with a stern expression, "ID please!"

Xu Hu responded, "He's coming to my

home."

The sentry maintained his silence and his ramrod posture.

Xu Hu urged me, "Let's go in. This is the living quarters of the department chiefs and directors and above. That's why there is a separate sentry here."

I followed her without a word, my pace visibly slowing down. I hadn't imagined her father was a high official at such an elevated rank. Heads of departments in a greater military region normally would at least be a deputy chief of staff, with the rank of a corps commander, such as a general. I had a hard time trying to figure out the tone with which to address her father.

In the compound there were a dozen red-tiled two-storied buildings, probably housing two families each as every building had two doors. The buildings were not particularly outstanding in architectural aesthetics but they were surrounded by trees and flowers as in a park setting. I tried to guess which building was Xu Hu's home and imagined the furnishings inside, but she turned right and entered a quiet alley bordered by oleanders. After walking a short distance, we came to the end of the alley and the entrance of another walled compound. This small compound within the compound that was within the compound was also guarded by a sentry, who evidently knew Xu Hu very well. He smiled at Xu Hu and did not demand to see my ID.

There was nothing small about this "little compound;" a western-style detached house stood at the center of a sizeable lawn, much more imposing than the other buildings.

I did a double take, "Your father is …?"

"The deputy commander."

"Of the greater military region?"

"Yes."

I followed her as she walked toward the house while talking. If I had known her father was the deputy commander of the military region, I probably wouldn't have come with her. But there was no turning back now.

Inside, the furnishings of the deputy commander's home were astonishingly modest. Today people probably think I am exaggerating about what happened twenty years ago. Even in those days it was beyond belief unless you saw it with your own eyes. The garden was exquisite. The house was gorgeous. But inside the house there was almost nothing. The most presentable room was the living room downstairs, furnished with a set consisting of one old fabric-faced sofa and four smaller chairs, which looked so forlorn in this cavernous room, which could hold two hundred guests for a ball.

"Please have a seat," said Xu Hu.

I remained standing.

She laughed, "Relax, my folks are not home."

"Really?"

"One went down to inspect troops and the other went back to the home town."

Relieved, I sat down on the sofa and said, "So that's why you thought it safe to bring me here."

"You may be afraid of them. I'm not. Want to take a tour?"

"Of course, this will be educational. It may come in handy one day if I decide to write a play about generals." I began to relax.

"There's really not much to see. We don't have much in the way of furnishings," Xu Hu explained as she walked up the stairs.

She did not lie. The furniture consisted uniformly of military-issue camping gear made for the barracks. The crudely made tables, chairs and stools would fit in an equally crude barracks, but transplanted to a garden villa, they looked out of place and unharmonious. As if this were not enough, even these crude articles of furniture were few and far between. Every room in the villa was immense, and in every one of these large rooms, only a few necessary pieces of furniture were found, such as a table, chairs, and a plank bed. There were no big armoires or wardrobes. Clothes were stored in canvas trunks. In Xu Hu's room there was not even a canvas trunk and her clothes were stored in three soap boxes. I suddenly remembered Xu Hu's cloth shoes which were so in character with the furnishings of her home.

One of the rooms was locked. Xu Hu said it was her father's office. "Even I am not allowed to enter this room," she said. "Nor my mother." I peeked through the keyhole and saw a double-barrel hunting gun on the wall. That was the only thing I saw that befitted, in my imagination, the status of a deputy army commander.

Since her parents were not home at the time of my visit, the significance of the invitation changed radically from what I'd imagined. I got a funny, mixed feeling. On the one hand I was a little disappointed; on the other hand I was glad it had turned out the way it did. It suddenly occurred to me that it could all have been carefully planned by Xu Hu. She was trying to acclimatize me, cushion me psychologically, so to ease me through the transition. She was really a very smart girl.

Five

It started to get dark. Shapes became a little blurred and indistinct before my eyes.

"It's hard to imagine," said Xu Hu, "that 22 years have gone by."

"Yes, twenty-two years."

"Frightening. I will soon be 40, I feel so old."

"No, you are not old."

Xu Hu laughed, "You are just humoring me. Still treating me like a seventeen-year-old girl, are you?"

"No, I'm serious; you are not old. You are as pretty as you ever were." I was sincere.

She laughed again, "The room is dark; that's why you can't see the wrinkles on my face."

Contemplating her, I had an impulse to get up and turn on the floor lamp so that I could have a closer look at her. But I restrained myself. Reason and sentiment, and reason and desire rarely mix well. I did not want to indulge my impulse only to regret it later. Nothing could come of it, so why not preserve a pleasant, unsullied memory for both of us. The male sex does not have the luxury of getting carried away by emotion.

Looking up at me, she asked, "Don't you want to take a closer look at me?"

"I already did. As I said, you are as pretty as ever."

The observation seemed to lose some of its sincerity when repeated.

She appeared to sense something and asked, "You have not been ... doing so well?"

"I'm fine," I replied.

"I know you are not fine."

"Why, do you hope I'm not doing fine?"

I laughed.

Looking at me, she seemed on the verge of tears.

I quickly suggested, "Why don't we go somewhere and have some fun."

"All right," she said, "what fun things can we do?"

"Right, that's a good question. I'm no expert on fun things."

"What about karaoke?"

"You really expect someone with a cracked voice like me to sing karaoke?"

"A cracked voice is cool nowadays."

I laughed, "Or we could dance."

"You've learned to dance?"

"What do you mean?" I said. "You sound as if I could never learn how to dance."

"Let's do it then."

"But … to tell you the truth I am not too good at dancing. Don't curse me if I step on your toes."

She laughed, "Never mind, let's go to a restaurant instead."

"Yes, let's." I really felt hungry.

I did not eat much. I spent most of the time watching her eat. The way she attacked her food brought up a host of memories. As in the past, she ate with gusto, relishing every bite even if it was the humblest vegetable. I believe that the way one eats reflects one's attitude toward life, whether one is positive, engaged with society and full of life and spirit.

The restaurant, which offered "benbang" (local) food, was doing a brisk business. "Benbang" food, or local cuisine, was all the rage in Shanghai recently. Xu Hu said that "benbang" food was also popular in Beijing. I asked if she meant the local Beijing cuisine. She said no; "benbang" food always referred to Shanghai cuisine in Beijing. I said that was interesting; how could the Beijing natives be so imprecise in language use? "Benbang" food in Beijing should be designated as Beijing cuisine.

Xu Hu laughed, "You are ever so strict

with words."

I also laughed.

In a crowded public environment, everything felt more relaxed and spontaneous than when we were alone in the privacy of the hotel room. This is peculiar in a large metropolis. I made an unexpected discovery that eating in the big public space of a restaurant created a much healthier mood than if we were sat in one of those private rooms. In the public hall the diners' buoyant moods combined to form a boisterous, euphoric atmosphere, in which the anonymous strangers went about their gastronomic business, free of the unwanted intrusions of privacy.

Xu Hu raised her head, her mouth still gracefully chewing. "Why have you stopped?"

"I've had a lot."

"You didn't eat much. You think I haven't noticed anything because I'm so absorbed in my food?"

"Of course you have a talent for multitasking, as always."

She laughed with pleasure, "But you don't need to scrimp and save as in the past to feed me; now we can eat to our heart's content."

"But you still look as if you had gone without food for three days."

"Is that true?" She let out a loud laugh. "I really enjoy eating. I can't help it."

I was feeling closer to her. The past began to come back in waves, not in the form of specific events but of the feeling of togetherness. Twenty years of distance suddenly was reset to zero. My hope was all of a sudden revived. Could we pick up from where we left off? But I immediately ordered myself to bury the thought. It was another illusion, no doubt about it! I must remember that twenty years of our lives could hardly melt away like ice sculptures, without leaving a trace.

She put down her chopsticks and said

with a sigh of satisfaction, "Now I am full."

"More dishes are coming," I said.

"I will continue in a while. Do you smoke?"

"No. Do you?"

"Yes."

"Go on, take a smoke."

"Never mind."

"Why not? Smoking is not prohibited here."

"I don't want to ruin your perception of me."

"What perception?"

"I'm sure you've been recalling what I looked like when I was younger."

I nodded. "But I don't have a strong objection to smoking."

She fished out a cigarette from her purse and lit it. She didn't look too bad when she smoked; in fact she looked quite charming.

"I decided not to ask, but now I can't resist the urge," she said. "You don't need to answer if you don't feel like it. Are you single?"

"Yes."

"Divorced?"

"Yes."

"And the grounds for your divorce?"

"Let's drop the subject. It's all in the past now," I said. "Can we not talk about it?"

"All right." She called the waiter, "Check please."

"This will be my treat," I announced.

"Fine," she replied.

We emerged from the restaurant into a wide street in a newly developed zone in the Hongqiao district. Xu Hu suggested that we go back to her room.

After some hesitation, I said, "Let's call it a day. I'm going home."

"Still have something planned for the evening?"

"No."

"Aren't you single? Why the hurry to go home?"

I didn't know how to answer the

question.

"All right, bye then." She turned and left.

Once home, I didn't know how to occupy myself. It was useless trying to read. Surfing the channels on the TV, I couldn't find one show that I could stand for any length of time. I could not stop thinking about her. My mind was full of her. At the end of my emotional tether, I found the number of the Galaxy Hotel by dialing 114, the directory assistance number.

"What are you doing?" I asked.

"Nothing."

"Have you been thinking about me?"

"Why should I be?"

"Are you mad at me?"

"Why should I be?"

A pause intervened.

"Xu Hu, maybe I presumed too much. I was afraid that if I went back to your room, I would be unable to control myself."

"You … want to? With me … I mean?"

"I do."

"Then why … aren't you single?"

"But you are not."

"I'm married in name only."

"Really?" I said in astonishment. "What happened? Why?"

"Can one ever explain why? You didn't tell me why either."

"Then are you planning to … part?"

"If there's no one to replace him, what difference does it make?"

We seemed to have come to a dead end in the conversation. I held the phone in my hand, hearing only the humming of electric currents. Then I heard her say, "Ting dear, want to come over?" It was almost an indecipherable sound, but I heard it clearly and distinctly.

Six

We had simultaneously come to the conclusion, as if by previous agreement, that we should avoid any discussion of her family. She refrained from mentioning her father or mother in my presence, and I refrained from asking. Our relationship remained basically the same as before. I had hoped that our relationship would undergo a fundamental change in its nature after meeting her family, but that was before the visit to her home. Once I knew her pedigree and the prominence of her family, I naturally stopped taking the initiative. I left the matter of any further development in the relationship up to her and her family. In a sense courtship is a war. The balance of forces between the two parties in our war tipped from one moment to the next, leaving a bitter taste in my mouth. Before this happened, I was superior to her in experience, capabilities and knowledge. I was a big brother that she looked up to and adored. She was still very nice to me and her respect for me had apparently not changed. Still, I had changed; more than before I took advantage of every possible opportunity to flaunt my knowledge and learning. When we talked, she was almost given no opportunity to put in a word sideways. Every discussion ended with my definitive, conclusive opinion. My posture as a strongman was very obvious, if not overdone. If Xu Hu found it overdone and exaggerated, she didn't tell me.

I would still sit by the window of my office, looking out through the foliage of the magnolia and the pomegranate trees at Xu Hu and others in basic skills practice. When I did, I no longer could concentrate on my reading or writing. I would think about what I was going to say to Xu Hu when she came over that evening, whilst before no prior thinking was ever needed. Unscripted and unprepared, our meetings used to be relaxed and spontaneous. Now they felt artificial and I didn't like it a bit. I tried, without success, to make things go back to the old way.

About two or three months later, the director of the cultural service called me into his office. After closing the door, he asked, "Did you volunteer to transfer out of this unit?"

I was dumbfounded. "What transfer?" I asked.

"You didn't put in the request? Okay, I'll talk to personnel. That's all, you can leave."

I didn't leave. I asked my supervisor where I was supposed to be transferred to.

My supervisor said, "Might as well tell you. If personnel should want to talk to you directly, you can make known your choice.

You are to be sent to a training school for military cadres. Damn! They don't know what they are doing. They could easily find a company commander or staff officer anywhere, why are they trying to pry away the valuable writing talent we've discovered after so much trouble. Personnel people always give short shrift to cultural work."

It was so unexpected for me; such a rude shock. After leaving the office of my supervisor, I went directly to personnel on the second floor. At the door of the personnel office I waved to Liu Yue inside. He followed me downstairs and said to me when we stopped just outside the small grocery store nearby, "You should have called instead of coming here in person."

"Why?"

"People in my office know that you and I are from the same town."

"Why does that matter?"

"Are you playing dumb or what? Aren't you trying to find out about your transfer?"

"Of course."

"By showing up in my office, you are basically telling everyone that I, Liu Yue, have discipline-defying, liberalistic tendencies."

"Oh," I said, "I should have been more careful."

"It seems you are only good as a soldier; you don't have any political smarts."

I seized on the theme and asked, "Why this sudden decision to transfer me to a military training school? What's the reason?"

Liu Yue replied, "That's what I wanted to ask you. It's the political commissar who personally arranged your transfer. Since when does a corps-level chief officer take a personal interest in someone with a rank equivalent to a deputy company commander like you?"

It instantly dawned on me. It was Xu Hu's father; it must be Xu Hu's father who intervened, although I couldn't fathom why her father would want me to study in a training school for military cadres.

"Hey, I am asking you!" said Liu Yue. "How did you all of a sudden find yourself a friend in such a high place?"

"If I knew, would I have come to you for enlightenment?" I decided to play dumb.

I was desperate to see Xu Hu, but she happened to have been sent on a tour to perform for the troops. During the three days before her return, I mulled over the situation I faced. On the whole the prospect looked good. At least, it meant Xu Hu had talked to her parents about us. By seizing the initiative she had shown that our relationship had now advanced to a higher plane. This was my first conclusion. Second, it seemed her father had given his consent to, or at least reluctantly accepted our relationship; otherwise he would not have taken an interest in my future. Judging from his attitude toward our relationship based solely on his daughter's description, I concluded that he clearly was an enlightened old man concerned about the well-being of the younger generation. I began to imagine what he looked like and what would happen when I formally presented myself at his home. Those imagined scenes took on an air of authenticity when replayed many times in my mind.

On the third night, Xu Hu and her troupe returned by about nine o'clock. The quiet compound instantly came to life; some started eating their evening snacks, others took showers and there was general laughter and merriment as if it had been New Year's Eve. I sat before my window, watching Xu Hu walking back and forth. I was sorely tempted to pull her into my room. She would absolutely not have the courage to come straight to my room upon her return, especially with so many people about, even though our relationship had been public knowledge for some time now.

But if she didn't come now, it would soon be taps and everybody would supposedly be in bed. It would then be harder for her to come to my room. I was in agony. I started pacing on the uncovered balcony, with my head lowered and hands clasped behind me, ostensibly thinking and conceiving a piece of writing; in reality I was trying to attract her attention. The band conductor came up to me, banging on his wash basin, and said. "Stop pacing. Go inside. I'll act as your messenger."

Xu Hu's face was flushed when she came in, either because she just came out of a shower or out of embarrassment. I had never found her so pretty.

She wrinkled her nose and said with feigned anger, "You are so impatient!"

She glared at me before breaking into laughter. I felt an instant relief. It seemed we had reverted to our spontaneous old times. I had an impulse to take her in my arms and kiss her. But I checked myself and asked,

"Did you mention us to your father?"

"How did you know?"

"I was notified by personnel to report to a training school for military cadres."

"Training school for military cadres? What for?"

"I guess ... but I could be wrong ..."

"No ..."

"What?"

"He is against your involvement in cultural work."

"Why?"

Idly flipping the pages in an issue of PLA Art and Literature, she said, "Just ignore him."

"What did he say?"

"Hey, there's a group of poems by you in this issue!" She enthused.

"Yes."

"Why didn't you tell me?"

I shrugged, "It was no big deal."

"Hey, it's PLA Art and Literature no less," she said, "it's no mean feat to get a piece published in PLA Art and Literature."

I persisted, "What did your father say?"

"What could he say? He is fundamentally contemptuous of art and literature. He says only soldiering is proper work. Exactly the type of simplistic military perspective criticized by Chairman Mao."

"Why did he let you work in the cultural field then?"

"That's what I asked him. He says he has no quarrel with women singing and dancing, but it's not something for a man who wants to go places or be somebody."

I felt insulted. I found it incomprehensible, unthinkable. "Did he really say that? He couldn't have; he is in a leadership position…"

Xu Hu said with a snort, "He may sound like a stalwart Marxist-Leninist when he delivers an official lecture, but deep down he is very feudal."

"That can't be true …" I said without conviction, as a Mao quotation came to my mind. "An army without culture is a dull-witted army." For me literature was my life's work, a sacred cause, an ideal that I was not prepared to abandon simply because of the prejudice of someone, even if that someone was a general, even if it was Xu Hu's father.

Looking at Xu Hu, I said, "You won't be upset if I do not heed your father's advice?"

She said, turning her head sideways, "Did I say I wanted you to heed his advice?"

"What did he say about us?" I asked.

"What about us?" she retorted teasingly.

"I don't know."

"I don't know either."

I picked up that day's Sichuan Daily, with a headline news item on its first page about Jiange County building terraced rice fields modeled on the Dazhai experience. Xu Hu yanked the paper away and asked, "Are you upset?"

"No."

"Can't I tease you?"

"I didn't say you couldn't."

"Look at the face you put on! I was kidding because I was happy."

"Did your father give us his blessing?"

"Why else would he take an interest in your career?"

"What exactly did he say?"

"He didn't say anything."

"Nothing?"

"Why can't you think properly whenever it comes to something that concerns you personally? How can he openly give his approval? Even a commander in chief has to respect army regulations."

"Then why did he think he could meddle in the affairs of the political department?"

"He did it because he thought it was in your interests."

I fell silent. But I must say Xu Hu was right.

A few days later the cultural troupe traveled to eastern Sichuan to entertain the troops there. When their truck left the compound, I suddenly discovered that

Xu Hu did not go with the troupe but was standing at the gate waving goodbye to her comrades.

"Why aren't you going?" I asked.

"I sprained my ankle."

I asked anxiously, "What happened? Is it serious?"

"It's nothing serious. The political commissar insisted on keeping me here after overhearing me casually mention the incident."

Lao Zhang the gate guard interrupted, "Go back in. I am closing the gate."

It suddenly occurred to me that besides Lao Zhang, who lived in the gatekeeper's cabin, there were only the two of us in the entire compound. We would be together, day and night, the whole ten days. We could do whatever we liked and nobody would disturb us. My heart started to race and my face burned. When we walked back, my hands and legs felt stiff and awkward.

Xu Hu, probably also sensing this

change, followed me without a word, her head bowed. When we reached the door of my room, she kept on walking. "Aren't you coming in?" I asked.

She went in, still standing and her head still bowed.

"Why don't you sit down?"

She sat down, her face becoming redder by the second as if blood would break out of her skin at any moment. I wanted to touch her face; it must have been burning hot. But I didn't move; I just looked at her. The room was very quiet. The thought occurred to me then that the political commissar must have kept Xu Hu home deliberately. He must have known who Xu Hu's father was. He must also know about Xu Hu and me. Whatever the reason for his special arrangement, I was sincerely grateful to him.

I was emboldened by the thought that this opportunity of being alone together with Xu Hu had seemingly been officially sanctioned and therefore was legitimate.

I asked, "How's your ankle?"

"It's nothing."

"Let me take a look."

"Go ahead."

I pulled my stool closer to her and said, "Put your foot here."

She meekly put her foot on my lap. I touched the ankle gently, "Is it here?"

She nodded.

"Does it hurt?"

"No."

"Let me take a look."

She didn't say anything.

I gingerly removed her shoe and slowly peeled off the cloth sock, revealing her white, smooth, delicate dainty foot. I'd never seen her bare feet before and had long yearned for a look, only I had been too embarrassed to ask. From the appearance of her hands I had extrapolated what her feet would look like, but the foot before me now was far more appealing than anything in my imagination. I would never have imagined a woman's foot could be so delicate and slender and yet so "fleshy." The most seductive part was the pink heel, rounded and supple, going up to the delicate ankle in a charming curve. I stroked her foot, from the toe to the sole, on to the heel and up to the ankle, again and again, in endless repetition. I was in a state of trance and intoxication, marveling at this exquisite masterpiece. I couldn't resist the urge to bend down and plant a kiss on the back of her foot. She pushed my head away and said rebukingly, "It's dirty."

"No, it's not dirty. Your foot is fragrant." I couldn't raise my head because I was kissing every inch of her foot from front to back. Her eyes were closed and her hands rested on my shoulders; I could feel she was shaking all over.

Suddenly she thrust me away a second time. Afraid that I'd upset her, I was going to offer some kind of explanation when she asked, "Do you want to look at me?"

I did not answer, realizing what "look at" meant. I was of course eager to "look at" her, but how would I dare to say it out loud? Not long before, a soldier from Shaanxi who worked in the kitchen of the cultural troupe was given a demerit after being found to have been peeking into a women's shower room.

Without waiting for an answer, she got to her feet and made her way to the window and pulled the curtains shut. She stayed by the window, without turning around, with her back to me, and began to unbutton her blouse, slowly, without hurry or nervousness. I was stunned; I hadn't expected her to be so bold, to take the initiative … I felt like I was in a dream. I watched, eyes bulging, and with bated breath. I could hear the thumping of my heart.

That day, I caressed every inch of her body, with my hands, my eyes and my lips. Since then I have never again fondled another woman with as much devotion, abandon and tenderness, or taken so long in doing it. She was the first woman I'd ever caressed and the most beautiful in my mind's eye, because she was the woman I loved.

We lost track of time; by the time we were done, the dark of night had enveloped us.

But all I did was caress her, that day and the rest of the ten days. As much as I yearned to break that last barrier, I didn't. I controlled myself; I did not betray any outward sign of this desire. In those days, both she and I considered the virginity of a young girl to be something sacred. Since I loved her, I had to respect her.

Even though that was all we did, those ten days were like heaven, but heaven was so short-lived.

Seven

The next afternoon, Xu Hu called, "Can you come out now?"

I said yes. She gave me an address on Hongqiao Road and asked me to go there immediately. "What's it about?" I asked.

"You'll know when you get there."

I hesitated but she already hung up. I didn't want to go but had no choice because I didn't have her beeper and cell phone numbers and therefore couldn't get in touch with her.

The night before I had gone to her room in the Galaxy Hotel. I knew before I arrived what would happen. Both of us knew, without spelling it out, we were going to do "it." But it didn't work out. I didn't do it. I didn't think I would fail to perform, but I just couldn't do it.

"That's all right," she tried to comfort me. "Let's not rush it. There's always a period of mutual adjustment."

I said nothing.

"Haven't you had a woman after your divorce?"

"No."

"You are such a virtuous person. No wonder you are out of practice."

She was trying to cheer me up, to make me laugh. But I didn't laugh.

"Relax. It will be better when you are relaxed."

"I can't relax."

"Why? Are you concerned about the chamber maid barging in without knocking?"

I nodded.

"It won't happen. This is a big hotel, not one of those crummy guesthouses."

"I still feel uneasy."

I began dressing, as did she.

"It's all right," she said after getting dressed, "sex is not the most important thing to us, don't you agree?"

Yes, I said. But I thought to myself, if there was no sex, what would be left between us? I regretted having come. I should have resisted coming to the hotel. At least, we would have salvaged some fond memories. Now, even those memories were tarnished.

I didn't know how I could face her again. Would we be able to act naturally with each other from now on?

Although I drove to Hongqiao Airport a lot, I had never been aware of the existence of this elegant neighborhood of newly built detached houses in this part of Shanghai, as it did not adjoin any major roads leading to the airport. It is often said that even when they build detached houses, the Shanghainese are stingy with space. Not true. As long as you have money, you can build houses with the most generous proportions.

Xu Hu sat in a chair on the large balcony in front of the house, made bright and beautiful by the winter afternoon sun.

"Come!" She called to me and affectionately pulling me to her side.

Reflexively I looked about.

"Don't worry. Nobody will see us."

It was true. The house was surrounded by trees; all neighboring houses were well hidden behind trees. I wondered how it was possible that the houses were newly built and yet the trees around them had already grown to such heights.

"Is this a hotel?" I asked.

"No, it's not a hotel. It's all private houses. Come in and take a look around."

Of course it was nicely appointed. I couldn't find anything bad to say about it. But I couldn't shake off the impression of a hotel, one of those high-class, villa-style resort hotels. Why else would the interior not show any signs that it had ever been lived in?

"Did you rent it?" I asked.

"Yes."

"From whom?"

"Why would you care? It will be ours for a few days. We won't be bothered by anyone."

I stared at her, speechless.

"Why are you staring at me? Don't you believe me?"

"No, it's not that I don't believe you … Just because I said yesterday I felt uneasy, you have …"

"You are right. I want you to feel at ease as if you were in your own home."

I laughed, "But I don't feel at home at all here. My home could never be so elegant."

"I mean security, privacy, the ability to do as you like as in your own home."

I nodded. She was trying to rebuild my self-confidence, to salvage our relationship. Obviously she was serious about it. I was touched by this kind of seriousness in someone who had reached her age. I was touched, even if nothing might have come of it.

"Xu Hu."

"Yes?"

I wanted to say "thank you," to acknowledge her kindness. But I said nothing. Anything I said would sound as stilted and insincere as language in a script. On the other hand I did have the feeling that we were acting out a scene in a theatrical piece.

The light began to fail in the room. The lamps remained turned off. We were so exhausted we did not seem to have the energy to turn them back on.

"Was it okay?" I asked.

"It was very good. Unexpectedly good."

"I didn't expect it to go so well either."

"You lied to me."

"What did I lie about?"

"You told me you didn't have a woman after your divorce."

"You wouldn't mind, would you?"

"Wouldn't mind what?"

"That I had … that I had other women."

She shook her head.

"Do you now?"

I shook my head.

"I don't mind if you do."

"I really don't."

"Then … why did you and your wife break up?"

"Because she found someone better."

"So she chucked you out?"

"You might say that."

"What a letdown. I thought …"

"What did you think? Nowadays many women initiate divorce."

"I'm not talking about who initiates it. I thought … I thought you were divorced for my sake."

I couldn't make out her expression in the dark. I couldn't be sure if she was kidding or she was truly disappointed.

She lit a cigarette, which cast a weak,

flickering light on her face. But I still could not clearly see her expression.

I said, "When it comes down to the real reason for my divorce, I have to say it was you."

She laughed.

"Why did you laugh?" I asked.

"You don't need to comfort me," she replied.

"I'm not trying to comfort you," I said. "Do you know why I married her in the first place?"

She said nothing. I had a feeling she was watching me.

"Give me a cigarette."

"Do you smoke too?"

"Occasionally."

I lit the cigarette and continued, "Soon after being discharged from the military, I went to work in a factory; then I was transferred to a government office. When I worked in the factory, a lot of people tried to match me up with different women.

None worked out. When I began work a few years later in the government office, I was immediately attracted to a typist in our unit. Before long we got married. The reason I found her attractive was that she resembled you."

"Really?" she said in a raised voice.

"I did not realize it at first. In my memory you were this girl in military uniform with short hair; she, on the other hand, wore civilian clothes and sported long hair, so I didn't immediately connect you with her. I only found her pleasant and pleasing, and took a liking to her. Several months after getting married, she cut short her long hair in summer and suddenly she reminded me of you. I realized then that I grew fond of her because of you. Maybe it's the bad habit of a writer, but from then on I constantly compared her to you. Whenever something happened, I would think what you would do if you were her ... She didn't survive the comparisons."

"I would not necessarily have turned out better than her. You believed I was better because you did not get to marry me. The things you want but don't possess are always more desirable."

"Yes, that may have been a factor."

"So you just parted like that?"

"It didn't happen that quickly. The relationship didn't sour overnight. But something didn't feel right. Later ... she found another man. I did not blame her. We parted calmly and amicably. I've always felt I was partly responsible."

"I'm sorry."

I laughed, "Why should you be sorry?"

"Don't you have kids?"

"No."

"You've been celibate ... for a long time?"

"For several years now."

"And you've been single all through that period?"

"Yes, single all that time."

"Why didn't you find another woman?"

"I got scared," I said. "Once bitten twice shy."

She didn't pursue the subject. I too kept silent. We lay there without saying anything. It was quiet around the house. So quiet you could make out the sounds of cars traveling on Hongqiao Road quite some distance away. The sound of tires rubbing against the road surface, filtered through rows upon rows of trees, was as soft as the whisper of drizzling rain. I was in a good mood, mainly brought on by regained self-confidence. Whatever barrier had existed between us had been blown away in the cathartic, liberating battle that ended a short while ago.

She lit another cigarette and finished it in silence. Extinguishing the stub, she said, "Uh-oh."

"What?" I asked.

"I'm hungry."

I laughed.

"Don't laugh. You will feel hungry soon enough."

"I am already."

"Why did you laugh then? Let me warn you. This is not a hotel and there's no food."

"Have money, will eat," I said. "Let's call a taxi and go to a restaurant."

"I can barely get up."

"All right, I'll go get some takeout food."

"That'll be wonderful. Buy a lot while you are at it. There is a fridge and a gas range. Get a lot of frozen food, noodles, eggs, bags of salted vegetables and snacks."
"How big a stomach do you have? It's only for two days."

"It can always come in handy later. I'll leave in two days but will be back again in a few days."

"A few days? You'll be back here in a few days?"

She said nothing.

"How long have you rented this house for?"

"I've rented it … forever."

"What?"

"This house belongs to us."

I switched on the lamp and momentarily blinded myself in the bright light.

"What are you doing?" she said.

"What did you say? This house belongs to us? Where did you get all this money?"

She laughed, "Stop making a big deal out of it. Of course I don't have that much money. The title to the house is held by my company, but we can live here for as long as we want. I am the chairperson of the board. What do you say?"

What could I say? What did "we" mean? Lovers? Husband and wife?

Eight

The matter of going to a training school for military cadres seemed to have been shelved. My supervisor never mentioned it again. Shortly after, I was sent to Tibet to experience life there. It was a painful parting for Xu Hu and me. After those ten days spent alone together, we seemed to have fused into one. It was hard for me to accept a long separation, not least because it was long both spatially and temporally.

The assignment to Tibet brought home to me for the first time the true meaning of distance. The Ilyushin Il-18 left the Chengdu basin and began to fly over mountainous terrain shortly after taking off from Shuangliu Airport. The mountains kept getting higher and bigger and more savage. They were vast arid mountains devoid of life. They separated me from China proper, from Xu Hu. Mountains and rivers were now barriers that made my longing for her so much more heartrending. It was almost unbearable for me. But I was a soldier, a man. I could not give up my life's work for the sake of romantic love. I was determined to produce a masterpiece that would make Xu Hu proud and make Deputy Commander Xu change his opinion of me. I must convert my longing for her into strength, into inspiration, into memorable, pithy words.

After a few days I gradually calmed down. The unique splendors of nature, the exotic customs and ways of life in Tibet and the legendary stories surrounding the troops stationed there did their share in relieving some of my angst and frustration. As I went about my journalist's business of conducting interviews, I was also conceiving a multi-act play centered on the theme of the united efforts of the Tibetan and Han ethnic communities, and of the military and the civilians defending national unity. The conception was going well and my reporting was reaping a bumper crop of information. I was driven by a creative impulse and expected to complete the first draft of the play during my stay at the Linzhi military guesthouse.

The guesthouse was a recently built low building of one story; its walls, floors and roof were all made from pine wood. As one walked into any of its rooms, one was enveloped by the rich aroma of resin. The windows opened out toward a vast stretch of cedar forest situated in a valley. These trees, which were considered a rare species in central China, covered the hills and fields of Linzhi. I felt privileged to be among them. There was a wool mill in Linzhi, which had been relocated here from Shanghai. Some Shanghainese staff in the mill had found out I was from Shanghai and began paying me visits at the guesthouse. We spent the time mostly chatting about our native city. Unexpectedly hearing so many people speaking one's own native dialect in a border town was a strange experience; it had a dreamlike quality. It warmed and gladdened one's heart, naturally. I vaguely sensed a new work in the making that would follow the completion of the play I was working on.

I took less than four days to finish the first act of the play. That evening Mr. Lei, chief of the reconnaissance section of the military subregion, knocked on my door and came in when I was reading out my play to a few newly met friends. I had met Mr. Lei in one of my interviews and we enjoyed talking with each other. I said he came at the right time because he could offer some comments on the play.

"Have you finished the whole play?"

"No, only the first act."

"You'll continue the writing in Chengdu?" said Mr. Lei.

"What? Am I going back to Chengdu?"

Mr. Lei did not respond. I glanced at the others in the room, who were all civilians, and followed him outside.

"The Air Force sent a cable through the Tibet Military Region and asked you to return to Chengdu immediately."

"Why?" I asked.

"I don't know. Soldiers follow orders; they don't need to know why."

My first thought immediately went to Xu Hu. Ah, I'm going back to Chengdu! I'll be reunited with Xu Hu! Longing, like a tidal wave, overwhelmed me. All of a sudden, I couldn't wait any longer. I wanted to fly to her side immediately.

I returned to Chengdu like a VIP. From Linzhi to Lhasa, I rode in a car specially arranged for me. From Lhasa to Chengdu I flew in a military transport plane, with me as the only passenger, so it was practically my personal plane. As much as I couldn't wait to get back to Chengdu, the special treatment first baffled and then unsettled me. I remembered the words of the chief of personnel; I thought of Xu Hu's father Commander-in-chief Xu. But when I boarded the plane, I dismissed those first thoughts. It would be inconceivable that they would dispatch a special plane to take a company-level officer to a training school for military cadres.

But what happened next was exactly as inconceivable. The chief of personnel said to me, "Xiao Zhou, you are to report to the cadres' training school tomorrow." I nearly doubted my sanity.

"After taking so much trouble to bring me back, you're ... sending me to a military cadres' training school?"

"What did you think you were called back for?"

If I had been completely in the dark, if I had heard this only from the chief of personnel, then it would have been an order of the hierarchy and I would have obeyed it. After all it's a soldier's duty to obey. But I already knew this hierarchy was none other than Deputy Commander-in-chief Xu and that this "order of the hierarchy" was based on prejudice and ignorance of art and literature.

Of course, all this was unknown to the chief of personnel. All he knew was he was carrying out an instruction from the top brass. If he had known the order came from the deputy commander-in-chief of the military region, he would have been doubly adamant on carrying it out.

"What did you say?" He looked fixedly at me. "You refuse to go? This is a decision made by the chief himself. How can you take such an attitude?" His eyes had an icy glint. If he had known the real reason for this decision, surely he wouldn't have looked at me like that. He would have been very kind to me. That's what went through my mind at that moment, but almost at the same time I felt ashamed of myself for the thought.

I was totally unprepared for this development. As much as I hated going to the training school for military cadres, as much as I couldn't bear the thought that I'd have to give up the multi-act play with only one act completed, as much as I did not take kindly to commander Xu's autocratic way of decision-making, I was not prepared to make a big stink in the political department and be forced out of the military as a result. Normally I was not one of those young hot-bloods unable to control their emotions or weigh their words. I repeatedly replayed the scene in my mind, after the fact, and tried to identify the reason for my abnormal behavior. I found out that the root cause lied in the fact that subconsciously I had placed myself in the class of "soon-to-be sons of high officials." It was very hard for me to swallow this bitter discovery. I'd always

despised those "sons of high officials" who
bullied others like "asses in lion's skin." They
were superficial and respected only money
and power. I never thought I would start
acting like an "ass in lion's skin" and even
before I had been formally admitted into
the club for the "sons of high officials." I was
shocked and dismayed by my own baseness.
The realization was deeply depressing.

I was directly taken to the political
department from the airport. I had not
yet seen Xu Hu and couldn't wait to see
her, although I felt some trepidation at the
prospect of meeting her.

My VIP treatment ended after my arrival
at the personnel department. Emerging
from the political department, I left the
compound of the corps headquarters and
started walking along the beltway toward
Sanshi village. I did not take the bus because
I wanted to take my time.

The rice plants by the highway had
started heading. Between the flowering of

the oilseed rape and the ripening of the rice plants, Xu Hu and I had been dating half a year. We got along very well. It would have been wonderful if she had been the daughter of ordinary parents.

I was not afraid of being discharged from the military. The Shanghainese soldiers all counted the days to their discharge. But if I were to be discharged now, what would happen to Xu Hu? Could she follow me to Shanghai? Would she?

I did not recount to Xu Hu my defiant behavior in front of the chief of personnel and the deputy chief of the political department. I simply said I was resigned to it, that it was my own fault. Xu Hu was naturally angry. She couldn't believe that I was facing discharge simply because I was unwilling to go to the military cadres' school.

"I'll go talk to my dad," she said. "He started the whole thing."

"No, don't go to him."

"Why not?"

"I don't want to owe anybody."

"Then you are ready for the discharge?"

I said nothing.

"What will become of me? What would happen to us?"

I remained silent.

"Pride is really so important to you? You don't care if you lose me because you are too proud to ask my father for help?"

I shook my head. I wanted to say, it was not pride, rather, it was low self-esteem. Before your father I would be such an insignificant person, a nobody. I was completely at your father's mercy. If I wanted to keep you, I had to pay the price of negating everything I stood for. That was too high a price to pay. I wanted also to say, my low self-esteem was also due to my realization that I was not as noble as you imagined me to be. I was not sure about myself; I didn't know what an obnoxious fellow I'd turn into if I became the son-in-law of a deputy commander-in-chief. I didn't want to be a despicable, unprincipled person chasing after power and money.

I said nothing.

Nine

I was beginning to get a hang of it. The size-11 ball was just right, not too heavy and not too light. When releasing the ball, I would cause the ball to spin with a twist of my fingers. A spinning ball had a much stronger impact on the pins. Occasionally I could knock down all ten pins in one throw.

The coach praised me profusely. I knew the praises were bought. Xu Hu had reserved a bowling room all to myself and hired a coach. Undoubtedly only the big bosses bowled in such grand style. So the coach was eager to please, but I suddenly lost my appetite for the game. Why should I practice to such stringent standards laid down by the coach? I was not planning on becoming a pro.

I had been called away from my office by Xu Hu. She wanted me to take her to an exhibition of Chen Yifei's paintings. As it was required by the exhibition, I went back home first to change into a suit before rushing to the Galaxy Hotel. But she said she still had some business to attend to, so I was to do a few games of bowling while waiting for her. She said it would be just a little while. The little while turned into nearly one hour.

I told the coach I wasn't playing anymore. Changing back into my street shoes, I dialed Xu Hu's cell number from a coin-operated phone in the hotel lobby. "I'm going back. There are some manuscripts that need my attention in my office."

"Where are you?" she asked.

"I'm in the lobby."

"I'll be there in three minutes."

I looked at my watch. Two and a half

minutes later, she emerged from an elevator. She headed toward me at a fast pace and asked, "Are you upset?"

"No."

"I'm sorry."

"No need."

"I really had to deal with something important at short notice."

"And I really have manuscripts to go through."

She laughed, "All right, all right, we'll leave this minute."

As we came out of the exhibition, Xu Hu asked, "Do you like Chen Yifei's paintings?"

I shook my head.

"Why not?"

"His paintings are commercial merchandise."

"And whose are not?"

"It's not the same. Although objectively all paintings have their value and price and can be merchandise, some paintings are born of the creative force of the artist, who does not give any prior thought to fame or money. These paintings were conceived as merchandise."

"What's wrong with that as long as the quality of the product is good?"

"I didn't say there's anything wrong with that. I only said I didn't like it."

"You said yourself you write sometimes to supplement your income."

"Yes, and that's why I don't like some of the stuff I write."

"You are really high-minded and have a lot of pride."

"Me? High-minded? Didn't I readily admit to writing for money?"

She smiled, "Your pride may have cost me a lucrative business deal."

I was startled. "You were discussing a business deal when I was bowling?"

"Uh-huh."

"How big was it?"

"Hundreds of thousands."

"It fell through?"

"Very probably."

"Why didn't you continue the negotiation?"

"You said you had to leave."

I was pleased. It appeared she cared about me. But I still said, "It would have been fine if we had each attended to our business. What was so important about an exhibition of paintings?"

"It was important to me."

"Then don't blame me for losing hundreds of thousands."

"I didn't blame you. I only mentioned it in passing."

In the taxi, Xu Hu asked, "Where will we go for dinner?"

"You decide."

"I don't know much about Shanghai."

"I know a lot about Shanghai, but not about its restaurants. People like us don't get to dine out a lot."

"Don't be snide."

The taxi driver interjected, "The Hai Ba Wang restaurant (the King Crab Restaurant) on Xietu Road is quite good, at 38 yuan per person. There are plenty of dishes to choose from and you can have as many helpings as you like."

Xu Hu asked me, "Have you ever been to the Hai Ba Wang?"

"I have."

"Is it good?"

"The common folks find the food decent and the price reasonable, but it's not exactly a high-class place. I don't know if it's up to your standards."

Xu Hu shot a dirty look at me. "Here you go again."

I was aware of the tartness in my remarks. It was unintentional; somehow they just blurted out. The subconscious mind is truly powerful.

The Hai Ba Wang, a huge two-level restaurant, was already full, with twenty to thirty would-be diners spilling into the street. It boggled the mind.

"Let's find another place," I said.

"No, this is it."

I laughed, "Don't do it to spite me. I misspoke a moment ago. You identify with the common folks, all right?"

"I'm not doing it to spite you. Many restaurants are now thinly patronized and yet business here is so brisk people have to line up for a table. They must be doing something right. I would have made a special trip to find out the secret of their success."

I looked at her. She was no longer the young girl doing songs and dances in the cultural troupe. She was a career businesswoman now.

She was as dedicated an eater as ever. She ate to her heart's content. I had to admit she did not exhibit any aristocratic tastes when eating was concerned.

"Are you done eating?"

"Yes."

"You were so consumed in eating. Did you learn the secret of their success?"

"Sure I did."

"What is the secret?"

She laughed, "The secret is they make a happy eater of me."

I also laughed.

"I'm not joking," she said. "The owner of this restaurant has found a way into the heart of his patrons."

She had a serious look on her face as she said this. It was then that I discovered quite a few creases at the corners of her eyes, thin but numerous.

"Where will we go in the afternoon?" she asked.

"It's up to you."

"Let's meet some friends of yours."

"Which ones?"

"Doesn't matter, as long as they are your friends. I should be introduced into your circles."

"By the same token I should be introduced

into yours."

"Right, of course."

"But I know next to nothing about you."

She laughed, "There's no hurry. I will disclose everything to you. But first let me go back to Beijing tomorrow to wrap up things."

"What things?" I asked. "You mean … getting a divorce?"

She nodded.

"Is it that simple? To get divorced, I mean."

"I don't believe it would be too complicated. I told you the relationship exists now only in name."

"How should I present you to my friends? As an old comrade-in-arms? A girlfriend? Or …"

"As your wife."

I laughed, "Yes, can I present you as my wife?"

"Yes, but more precisely, your wife-to-be."

As we walked by a branch of the Industrial and Commercial Bank, she handed me her bank card, saying "Do you want to withdraw some cash? The PIN number is 135246."

"Why?"

"When we meet your friends or later my friends, it will probably be better if you pick up the tab."

"I have cash." I handed the card back to her.

"Just keep it on you."

"I have cash."

"How much do you have?"

"Right now I have about a thousand on me."

"How much at home?"

"About three or four thousand in a savings account."

"That's not enough."

I cast a glance at her and went up to the ATM to withdraw three thousand yuan. Before making the withdrawal, I checked the balance in the account: seventy-five thousand yuan.

I handed the card back to her but she said, "You keep it. You'll get a card in your own name soon. It beats carrying cash on you. Counting cash is annoying."

Ten

The cultural troupe left on another tour. Before their departure Xu Hu pleaded with me not to do anything rash about my discharge before her return. I gave her my promise but the fact was I had already been called in for a meeting with my superiors and the matter had been decided. I just didn't have the heart to tell her. If she had known about it, she would have used her father's leverage to turn the whole thing around. She was capable of doing that.

When the truck left the gate, she smiled at me and I smiled back. But I felt a sharp pain tearing at my heart. I knew this could be our last farewell.

The compound was now quiet; there

was no more hustle and bustle, no more cacophony of strings, winds, contralto singing and crooning, laughter and chatter. Like the compound, my heart was drained, emptied. The last time, not so long ago, when the nest was emptied, the quiet compound was our Eden, with just me and Xu Hu. Today, the same compound had the eerie quiet of a graveyard.

Those special ten days in which Xu Hu and I were alone together seemed like only yesterday. I did not want to go over those ten days in my memory, but there was no way I could forget them. I saw Xu Hu everywhere; everything reminded me of her. There was no escape. I was escaping, I was leaving this place, but involuntarily, as if driven by unseen demons and spirits, I came to Xu Hu's dorm.

It was a well-kept girl's room. Xu Hu's bed was not by the window; as usual she'd left the most desirable spot for the others. It reminded me of the sterling qualities of Xu

Hu; I couldn't help thinking of her.

The bed was bare to the wooden bed boards, because the cultural troupe always took their own sleeping gear on their tours. Her underwear, socks and handkerchiefs hung on the headboard to dry. I brought my face close to the headboard to breathe in her body aroma deeply. During my last few nights in the military, I slept with her intimate clothing on my pillow, hoping to meet her in my dreams. I kept the underwear and socks until the morning of my departure then returned them to the headboard of her bed, but I took the handkerchief with a few plum blossoms printed on it with me as a keepsake.

Eleven

When we walked by the Pacific Department Store, Xu Hu insisted that we go in.

"What are you getting?" I asked.

"I want to get you some clothes."

"There's no hurry. I don't need to change to meet my friends. You'll have plenty of time to repackage me when you bring me into your circles ..."

She shot me a dirty look. I immediately zipped my lips, realizing that I misspoke again. What was the matter with me?! I had always believed I was not afflicted with pettiness. It turned out I was not immune to it.

We stood, like two rocks, amid the currents of passers-by heading in all directions.

"Then …"

"Let's go in," I hastened to say.

"What kind of clothes do you like?"

"I don't know." I really didn't know. I was too old to care about fashion. Or to put it another way, I lacked the incentive to care about fashion. I obviously had too negative a view of life.

"Get a suit. Those double-breasted ones with two rows of buttons are passé."

I looked down at the lapels of the suit I was wearing. "I rarely have an occasion to wear a suit."

"It's true you literary people don't normally need to dress up. But all the same get one. It may come in handy. For example when you meet people like Chen Yifei."

I laughed. We walked through the men's wear department. I had wanted to head straight to the suits section, but she made frequent stops to look at and touch merchandise that attracted her attention. I found that she was a connoisseur of apparel and fashion. Those articles that she liked invariably carried a hefty price tag. But I couldn't see the difference between those costing above a thousand yuan and those costing a couple hundred yuan.

We bought a lot of clothes. To be more precise, she bought a lot for me. I tried to appear enthusiastic. Whenever she had something good to say about something, I'd say I liked it too, although I really didn't. She was loaded with money and wouldn't care how much she spent anyway. Strange to say, she was buying clothes for me, but deep down I felt no pleasure and did not feel I should be grateful to her for what she did. Somehow I felt she was spending for her own sake, that she took pleasure in spending money and enjoyed the thrill of doling out favors. I don't know why the word "favors" crept into my mind. It was not the correct word to describe what she was doing. She was not doling out a favor to me; she bought those clothes for me out of genuine affection. It was I who was the morbid one.

When we emerged from the store loaded with shopping bags, she was truly very happy.

"I guess I don't need to change into another suit today, my friends …" I said.

"I didn't say you should change into another suit today. It's entirely up to you."

We returned to the Galaxy Hotel. She began to take a shower, apply makeup and try on one dress after another, while I busied myself making phone calls to round up my friends. Between phone calls she kept asking me, "How does this dress look? And this?" When I finished making my calls, she was still undecided as to which dress to wear. I had thought businesswomen would not spend an inordinate amount of time choosing a dress; apparently I had much to learn about women.

Her seriousness about the dinner

was contagious. I finally changed into a reversible casual shirt purchased that day, which appeared quite undistinguished at first glance. But if you looked closely at the stitch work, you'd find the fine workmanship that is the hallmark of famous brands. That kind of detail would probably be lost on my friends.

When introducing her, I still called her my old comrade-in-arms.

Xiao Ding from the Art Institute said, "It sounds funny when you call a pretty young woman an old comrade-in-arms."

Lin Tao from the radio station added, "What's so funny about that? I hope all Zhou Shuting's comrades-in-arms are pretty young women and that whenever a dinner gathering is planned we won't be left out."

There was general laughter. Xu Hu was also very happy. She kept repeating "thank you" and said that her appetite would be great today given all the nice things said about her.

"Shuting," she said, "why didn't you find a better restaurant?"

We were in a small restaurant noted for its continental European décor on Urumqi Road and the owner was a friend of Lin Tao's.

"The price is cheaper here, and we can get a discount," said Lin Tao.

Xu Hu looked at me, her eyes insistent.

"Where do you want us to go?" I asked her.

"Let's go to the Sea Palace."

"All right, let's go there."

I knew she was well-meaning and did it out of a desire to please and honor my friends. But none of us, who only moved in cultural and literary circles, would normally go to a place like the Sea Palace and be suckered by its Hong Kong owner. So she was as good as telling everyone that I was treating them to a dinner paid for by her. I wouldn't have much minded if she had announced up front that she would pay for the dinner. What bothered me was that I was supposed to pretend I was flush with cash by hosting this feast and by flashing the cash when it came time to pay the tab. I would be making a total fool of myself.

But everybody enjoyed the dinner, especially since they knew they were not eating at my expense and therefore did not feel indebted to me. Thus liberated and further loosened by alcohol, they began making jokes, naturally mainly at the expense of Xu Hu and me. These were close friends of mine and, encouraged by her frank and generous manners, they became more uninhibited as the conversation went on.

"You were dating already when you were in the military, right?"

"What if we were?" Xu Hu asked.

"What do you mean what if? You mean yes you were."

"Fine, we were," said Xu Hu.

"We can't let you off the hook as easily as

that. It's not enough to admit it. You must disclose the details."

"I can do that," Xu Hu said. "But you must agree to my conditions. For every detail I reveal, you must down a glass of rice wine."

Fine with us! No problem! Everyone got excited.

"It was in 1975 …"

"Wait! Wait!" Xiao Ding interrupted her. "How old were you in 1975? Did you join the military when you were only twelve or thirteen?"

"I wasn't only twelve or thirteen. I am 38 now."

"Nonsense! How can you be 38 already?"

"Would any woman deliberately overstate her age?"

"All right," Xiao Ding said, "let's assume you are 38 now. It means you were 17 in 1975. You dated already at 17?"

Xu Hu responded, "Quit being morality

police for the moment and drink your glass of wine first."

Xiao Ding protested loudly, "Did you count that as a detail?"

"Are you going to drink or not? If you don't drink that glass of wine, I won't continue the confession."

The others all said to Xiao Ding, "Drink it."

His eyebrows corrugated in anticipation of the 104-proof liquor, Xiao Ding downed a shot of Wuliangye, saying "Lao Zhou, you seduced a 17-year-old virgin. You are in big trouble."

Lin Tao shouted, "Stop interrupting. We want more of the confession."

"He wrote a play and I got a lead part in it."

"Wait! Wait! Wait!" Lin Tao said. "Here we need some clarification from Lao Zhou. Did you write the play with the express purpose of snaring her?"

"Yes, let Lao Zhou fill in the details." The

others joined in the chorus.

I just smiled, not in the mood to say anything. Somehow I'd lost appetite for the game. Xu Hu, sensing the change in my mood, said, "You want to hear him tell the story? Then I'll gladly pass the baton."

Lin Tao immediately said, "No, no. We want to hear it from you, of course."

Xu Hu said, "You showed disrespect for the key speaker by allowing your attention to drift. Don't you think there should be a penalty for that?"

"Yes, yes, there should be a punishment."

"Everyone drinks a glass of rice wine as punishment."

After drinking up his glass of wine, Lin Tao said, "Lao Zhou, your friend is really tough. I am no match for her."

That was how she got nearly everyone drunk, happily drunk.

Except me. My lips barely touched alcohol and remained mostly sealed.

On our way back, she asked me, "Are you upset?"

"No."

"I was just trying to entertain your friends."

"I know."

"It's not as if I'd said anything substantive."

"You're right and I did not fault you."

"But you didn't utter a word."

"I had too much to drink."

"You didn't drink much."

"I never was one to handle my alcohol."

Back in the house on Hongqiao Road, I offered to give the card back to her. "Why don't you pay in the future instead of through me; it is public knowledge that I'm spending your money anyway."

She pushed the card back toward me. "What are you doing? Isn't my money also yours?"

Yes, she could take that view, but I couldn't accept the idea. Even in the case of a married couple, property could be shared only if it was acquired after the date of marriage.

That night, we slept together again. Of course we truly went to sleep only toward dawn. Exhausted but satisfied, she fell fast asleep quickly. I was also spent but my head remained clear. I couldn't fall asleep and didn't want to. I had to admit we had a good time in bed. In the frenzy of passion, I never doubted for a moment that we would make a very happy couple. But after the tidal wave subsided, doubt sprang back as I looked out on the gray rooftops. I remembered what she said three days earlier: "Sex is not the most important thing to us."

I rummaged through her bag, fished out a cigarette and lit it. I smoked sitting up in bed with my back leaning against the headboard. She was still fast asleep. Her face, totally relaxed now, showed her age, which was less apparent during the day when she talked and laughed. I was assailed

by a sense that I didn't really know her. Did I
understand this woman? I had a passionate,
half-year romantic tangle with her twenty
years before; we got back together for three
days after a twenty-year separation. It was a
full twenty years of hiatus between the half-
year affair and the three-day reunion. Could
a twenty-year blank possibly be redeemed
by three days of togetherness?

I carefully went over in my mind the
three days we'd been together, trying to
reconstruct the sequence of life's events in
those twenty years. Although she did not
volunteer any detailed personal information,
it was obvious that she was the top dog of a
major company and was very rich, or had at
her disposal significant amounts of funds. If
it was the power wielded by her father that
separated us twenty years before, would
money be the barrier that was going to keep
us apart once again twenty years later?

I didn't know what to think ... no, not
true, I did know, but I was loath to admit

it. I'd always thought of myself as a high-minded, morally superior person, immune to the temptations of money. Could I still have the same certainty about my moral superiority after these three days?

I wished I could just abandon my claim to moral superiority, fall in love with money and dedicate myself to the pursuit of it without any complexities. Then I would have absolutely no reason to let Xu Hu slip through my fingers. Trouble was I couldn't bring myself to make a clean break from my high-mindedness. It was like chancing upon a treasure in the street. As much as I cherished it I would not dare put it in my pocket, because it had not been acquired after a long, hard quest but merely as a result of finding it by pure luck. Something found by pure luck does not truly belong to you.

That treasure lay before me now, within easy reach. She was returning to Beijing shortly to end her marriage. She was getting a divorce for my sake because she had made up her mind to marry me. Was I as committed to marrying her?

I didn't know!

I left quietly at the crack of dawn, leaving on the pillow the bank card and the handkerchief with a pattern of plum blossoms now worn thin and becoming indistinct. I had thought about leaving a letter but couldn't find the right words, so I simply wrote:

Goodbye, Xu Hu!

No Explanation Is Necessary

One

I didn't notice him the first day.

My father had just come out of surgery, still connected to an IV drip. Although he did not utter a sound, he was undoubtedly in great pain. The pathology report was not in yet and the jury was still out on whether the tumor was benign or malignant. At moments like this, people become too preoccupied to notice things that are of little concern to them. I was reading Bread upon the Waters, a novel by the American author Irwin Shaw, while keeping an eye on the changes in my father's facial expression and the state of the IV drip. I knew by experience that when you keep vigil over a patient, you need to bring along an entertaining book to while away the time. You don't want a book with a heavy subject that throws up endless hurdles that thwart your comprehension. It also shouldn't be one that drags you in through suspenseful twists causing you to become so transfixed by the plot that you forget your patient. Irwin Shaw's books are perfect for such an occasion.

The next afternoon, my father's condition stabilized and his face relaxed to a more serene expression; his breathing became less labored and more even. The IV drip was still slowly administering medication in metered amounts. I had finished Bread upon the Waters. Without another book to read, I went back to watching the monotonous dripping of the IV pump. Soon my eyelids started to droop, but I could not afford to fall asleep. I needed a jolt, or at least something to distract me. When I heard a ruckus coming from the hallway, I went out to see what was going on.

A large crowd, mainly of visitors and

nurse aides, gathered outside the door of a washroom half way down the corridor. As I approached the washroom, I was assailed by a strong stench and heard a heated discussion.

"What a daft lady! Why did she have to wash her hospital pants? She should have thrown them in the bin for soiled articles."

"She soiled her pants because of diarrhea caused by her medication."

"But she shouldn't have washed them here of all places. People wash their bowls and chopsticks in this sink."

At the door of the washroom, the stench became unbearable. An elderly woman in patient garb was washing some clothes there. In the deep sink floated yolk-like feces. I took a step back. A nurse came down the hall and said, "What's there to see? It's only human excrement. Get Lao Wei here!"

"Lao Wei is cleaning up the toilet stall. She also messed up the toilet stall," someone else said.

A frown creased the nurse's face and the only thing she could do was wait outside the door. Then someone said in a loud voice, "He's here. Lao Wei is here."

This was the first time he caught my attention. A little over fifty, rotund in a healthy sort of way, Lao Wei was the picture of joviality. Obviously he was a janitor; in these circumstances a janitor was no less important than the commander-in-chief of the three armed forces. The crowd parted to let him through.

"Lao Wei, please do a thorough job of cleaning up. We need to wash our dishes here."

"Disinfect the place."

"Don't you worry. I will make the sink as clean as the bathtub in your home, all right?"

"Hey! Am I taking a bath here? Go and get her out of there please."

Lao Wei responded, "She is already halfway done. Let her finish."

The crowd dispersed, leaving the mess to Lao Wei. I did not leave immediately but stood there a while longer, watching Lao Wei, who watched the elderly woman washing her soiled pants, without trying to rush her. He waited patiently without showing the least bit of annoyance. I took a liking to him; a liking and no more. I didn't know I would later take a far deeper interest in him.

It was past curfew time and I was unable to read even though a weak light was left on to facilitate the monitoring of the IV pump to which my father was still connected. The light was too dim for any serious reading. Father was already asleep and the IV bottle had an ample supply of fluid, so I felt there was no point sitting by the bed. I went out into the corridor, which was now deserted and illuminated only by a dim light. I saw light coming out of a small room all the way down the corridor. I sauntered toward the light source and found someone reading in the tool room. At the sound of my footsteps, he shifted the book aside. It was Lao Wei. He looked at me, querying me with his eyes as if to say "What can I do for you?" I hastened to say I was not asking for his help. He continued to look at me and, seeing that I had no immediate intention to leave, he put down his book and motioned me to sit down.

I noticed that he laid the book down first with the cover facing up but immediately turned it over so that I was unable to tell what kind of book it was. The quick maneuver would probably have escaped the notice of most people but as a novelist I had an eye for detail. Apparently he did not want me to know what kind of book he was reading; that meant he did not particularly want me to stay there. "Sorry," I said. "I see that I am disturbing you." As I turned to leave, he stopped me. "Why don't you stay for a while?" He must have sensed my quick assessment of the situation and decided not to make me feel awkward or to appear discourteous. Whatever the reason, this was clearly an intelligent, quick-thinking and well-bred man, not exactly the stereotype of a janitor. It was quite sad when one thought about it. He and I were of the same generation. Most people of our generation started out more or less on the same footing. It was only through circumstance and chance that some struck out on a different path and the disparities widened between us as time went on. Lao Wei was a case in point. If he had had different luck at some point in his life, he would have become an official in a responsible position, a scholar or anything.

With these thoughts coursing through my mind, I sat down.

I hadn't planned on striking up a conversation with him, so I was momentarily at a loss for words after I sat down.

He came to my rescue. "It's a lonely business to keep vigil by a hospital bed."

"It's depressing in a hospital setting after a while because you are surrounded exclusively by sick people. You may have become accustomed to it after working in the hospital for so long," I replied.

"I came recently," he said. "A little over a month ago."

"Oh, where did you work before? In a factory? Or were you temporarily unemployed?"

He smiled, apparently in tacit acknowledgment.

"Why haven't you gone home for the night?" I asked.

"I'm on night duty. Someone must stay here in case some mess needs to be cleaned up in a hurry. Like what happened this afternoon."

"You had your hands full this afternoon."

"It was not too bad. I swept up the filth, rinsed the sink several times and soaked the surface areas with disinfectant. It's mainly the filth. If you don't much mind the filth, you are okay."

I nodded, getting to my feet. "Continue your reading. I have to go back to my father."

Before my younger sister came to relieve me at about midnight, I went out a number of times into the corridor to get some air; I saw that the light in the small room remained on. I did not bother him again but watched from a distance. I found out that he read very slowly because it was a long time before he turned a page. Either he had some reading difficulty because of an inadequate education or the book was not for casual reading. Judging from the way he carried on a conversation, I didn't think he needed help from any literacy campaign. Then what kind of book was he reading? My curiosity was piqued.

Two

A few days later, my father passed through the trickiest stage of post-surgery recovery and the pathology report came back confirming that the tumor was benign. A heavy weight was lifted. Freed from having to keep a constant vigil over my father, I found time to go to the customs agency on a journalistic assignment and complete an investigative report based on my interviews there.

One day I was waiting at People's Square subway station to interview a young officer from the customs agency. He said he did not want to be interviewed at his work place, and recommended a place outside. Experience told me that he would be a cooperative interviewee, eager to confide. We were to meet at the subway station and proceed to the underground shopping arcade, where we would find a tea house or a café for our interview.

I was early, so I sat on a bench on the platform reading an evening paper, monitoring out of the corner of my eyes passengers descending the two staircases. As a person walked down the stairs, the first thing to enter my vision would be the feet, followed by the lower limbs, the thighs, the waist, the upper torso, and finally, the head. Based on the shoes, the pants, the upper garment and the person's gait and posture, one could make a good guess, before one saw the face, about the person's age, gender, upbringing and occupation. When you saw the face you would find out how good your guess really was. There were hits and there were misses; I found it to be an amusing game. Holding the paper but not reading it, I had a lot of fun testing my guesses and judgment. Then I saw him; it was Lao Wei.

I didn't immediately recognize him as he walked down the stairs. Before his face entered my field of vision, I saw, a pair of shiny shoes and a smart, well-ironed suit. "Shiny" and "smart" were inadequate expressions; everything on him was from a imported prestigious name brand. I would never have guessed it was him, but the face looked very familiar and I thought I must have seen him somewhere. Then it hit me and I was dumbfounded. His outfit was so out of place with his occupation as a janitor that all of a sudden he became an enigma for me. I was not sure whether I should greet him or not. Thanks to the paper I held in front of me, I was able to continue to observe him surreptitiously from behind it.

Unaware that he was being observed, he headed straight to the side of the platform for passengers traveling in the direction of Xinzhuang. Clad in his smart suit, he looked impressive. Soon his train pulled into the station and he left. I was half tempted to follow him onto the train and find out where he was going to get to the bottom of the mystery. Of course I didn't budge from where I was sitting. I couldn't leave because I was meeting someone; besides, what right did I have to tail him, to encroach on another's privacy? Bemusedly I gazed after the receding taillights of the train and suddenly laughed. He could very well be an official sent incognito by the Health Department on an undercover fact-finding mission; or an actor intent on fortifying his thespian skills by experiencing life; or he is in fact a janitor with a penchant for dressing up. What's it to me? Habits acquired through my occupation as a writer can be very stubborn sometimes.

The interview went well and it put me in a jovial mood, so I went out of my way to take out an order of chicken porridge, a favorite of my father's, at a Little Shaoxing

Restaurant. When I walked into my father's hospital room, the first thing that greeted my eyes was Lao Wei cleaning the floor with a big mop. He was doing a thorough job, mopping under every bed and saying apologetically, "Excuse me, excuse me, watch your feet …" He mopped using meticulous, energetic strokes and as he neared the door, he straightened up and was about to rinse the dirty mop when he saw me. He asked with a relaxed smile, "Visiting your father?"

I was the one who was a bit ill at ease as I replied a little too quickly, "Yes … Are you on the midday shift?"

He said he preferred the midday shift because that allowed him to sleep through the morning. He was in his usual rumpled work uniform. The earlier scene of a Lao Wei dressed in his sharp, shiny suit must have been a surreal dream, a mirage; it had not and should not have happened.

At Father's bedside I asked about

his wound and appetite, all the while wondering about this enigma of a janitor. I had dismissed the possibility of an official on an undercover mission or an actor experiencing life, but still had no idea what was he doing taking the subway in a smart suit?

Father liked the chicken porridge so much that he asked for more. I dissuaded him from a second helping, saying I would reheat some more for him in the evening. He asked if I was leaving now. I said not yet. He was cheered. I knew he would have preferred that I'd stay a while longer with him but he said, "You haven't had your supper. Go home." I said supper was no problem. There were eateries everywhere. Father told me to have my supper and come back later.

I returned to the hospital after having a bowl of beef noodles at a Yon-ho Soymilk Restaurant. Instead of going directly to Father's room I made straight for the room at the end of the corridor. The tool room door was ajar, so someone must have been inside. I presumed it was Lao Wei. But why did I want to seek him out? I had come involuntarily to his door, driven by an interest or personal curiosity in him. Curiosity is normal and necessary for a writer, but dropping in on him like this was somewhat presumptuous. Maybe it would be better to wait for more spontaneous circumstances. As I turned to leave, the door swung open and Lao Wei appeared. "Shall we go down to the garden?" he asked.

He didn't ask me what business had brought me to his door but straight away invited me to go to the garden, as if the meeting had been pre-arranged. It was already dark and the little garden was deserted. We sat down on a stone bench with a massive tree behind us, its branches hanging darkly and heavily above our heads.

"Go ahead, what's up?" he said.

I knew what he meant by that. My interest in him had been too obvious, so it was only natural that he would think I had some business to discuss with him. But what should I say? I didn't know what to reply.

"Go ahead and question me," he said. "I saw you in the subway station today ... I've nothing to hide. I've never done anything bad. My finances are clean ..."

I was mystified, "What did you say? What questions did you expect me to ask you? What do you take me for?"

"I don't know. I found that you had been watching me ... Are you from the Public Security Bureau? Or the National Security Agency? I've no idea ..." he mumbled with his head bowed.

Heavens! I didn't know whether I should laugh or cry. "I'm so sorry for having caused you alarm. I'm neither from the Public Security Bureau nor the National Security Agency. I'm ..."

His head snapped up and his eyes held

mine.

"I'm a writer. I have a professional habit of people-watching and like to imagine the colorful stories of people from all walks of life. I had no idea it would give you the impression that … I'm really sorry to have caused you so much trouble. I didn't mean to."

"Oh, no, it's all right." He was visibly relieved as he stood up. After taking a few steps toward the patient wards, he paused and said over his shoulder, "You must be eager to hear my story."

I didn't reply, embarrassed to say more.

He retraced his steps and sat down, "All right, here's my story."

Three

I'm sure you are a good writer, because you have sharp perception. You didn't take long to zero in on me, although I thought I did a good job of disguising myself in the hospital. It was when I saw you in the subway station that I became uneasy, believing then that I'd finally been found out. You must have been astounded to see a janitor transformed into a CEO type. I am an entrepreneur, rather, I was one. I am now nothing. I'm only a janitor …

You must also be a lao san jie (one of those who graduated from middle school in the first three years of the Cultural Revolution). Oh, so you enlisted in the military in 1968. I was not as lucky as you.

I graduated from junior high school in 1966 and was assigned to an agricultural production team in rural Jiangxi Province. I'll skip that part. There are many stories to tell from that period, but they would be typical of everyone else's experience. I was transferred out of the countryside early on and started out as a worker in a factory in the province's foreign trade zone, later I was promoted to do the work of a supervisor without the title and pay that went with the job. When the high school graduates previously sent to the countryside were returned to the cities en masse in a policy change, I was already working in Nanchang in the planning division of the foreign trade department of Jiangxi Province. For that reason I did not come back to Shanghai but chose to stay in Nanchang. I've not regretted my choice. The overwhelming majority of the graduates from Shanghai had left and those that stayed did well as long as they had the skills. The local authorities there recognized their talents and put these Shanghai graduates in responsible positions and many have become chiefs of departments and services. I don't think they would necessarily have risen as high if they had returned to Shanghai. One can never tell though. One's fate is unpredictable and works in mysterious ways. Take my example ...

Instead of going into government, I chose to go into business. An opportunity presented itself following Deng Xiaoping's famous 1992 tour of south China. Inspired by Deng's call for stepped up reforms, the foreign trade authorities of the provincial government decided to contract out two companies and I won the bid for one of them, becoming its CEO.

They were practically paying me to make a killing for myself. The trading companies of the provincial government had established export and import channels and I was already familiar with the running of those companies as a section chief for many years in the planning division. I had a vast network of connections working for me. Once I got the contract to run the company I did away with all the sloth and lack of accountability and other ills associated with the old "public trough" system; there was no reason I couldn't turn a profit. Soon the company was thriving. I got to pocket all the profit after fulfilling the pre-established quotas. I marveled at the ease and speed with which my fortune grew.

The problem was that it all came so effortlessly and money just fell into my lap. The thought of possible losses in business ventures never occurred to me. I gave little thought to contingency plans to deal with possible business failure. I would still be thriving now if it had not been for the financial crisis in Southeast Asia. Who would have thought that the four little dragons of Asia were to collapse all at once? Last July we were still basking in the euphoria of Hong Kong's return to China. The day it happened, Xiao Qiong and I were on Bangchui Island in Dalian. Oh, yes, I need to fill you in on some personal details. I will tell you everything on condition that you won't put the details in your writing unless you find a way to camouflage them so that people won't recognize me in your account.

My wife and I went to the same university—the Radio and Television University. As I told you I was transferred to the foreign trade office of Jiangxi Province early on. I liked the job very much and would be sad to lose it. So I attended the Radio and Television University while still holding on to my job. I attended classes two days a week. Most of the students there were in a similar situation; they had a good job but were there to earn a degree as a stepping stone to a better future.

On the day of enrollment I was a little

early. Leafing through the roster, I found that of the 48 in our class only two were from Shanghai. One was me and the other was Ye Zi, my future wife. The rest were all locals from Jiangxi Province. I did not leave after completing my enrollment because I was curious to find out about Ye Zi, the other Shanghainese in my class. As I waited for her to appear, I marveled at the sophistication and refinement of the Shanghainese, which could be seen even in the apt names they chose. The name "Ye Zi" sounded like "leaf," unpretentious, familiar and rolling so easily off one's tongue. In her case, "zi" was written as "zi" the color violet (two homophones in Chinese), which instantly added color and elegance to the name. Like most Shanghainese I was afflicted with an ingrained contempt for out-of-towners. As I had a preconceived bias in favor of a fellow Shanghainese, the moment she appeared I already found her easy on the eyes. In fact she was not bad-looking; she had clean, regular features.

I did not introduce myself to her that day. It would be silly to give her the impression that I couldn't wait to make her acquaintance. I was indeed in no hurry to make her acquaintance. After I went home, however, I couldn't stop thinking about her. I was already 31 and still unmarried; I did not even have a girlfriend. When giving serious thought to marriage, the Shanghainese normally would want to marry a fellow Shanghainese for smoother communication and more similar lifestyles. That's why in the factories moved from Shanghai to third-tier cities in China's interior, the Shanghainese employees tend to marry each other. This practice, as in the case of marriage in the physiological sense, is irrational. But it was the dominant trend some years ago. It was not easy to find a Shanghainese to marry outside Shanghai; it was harder in my case because I had lived and worked far away from places with a sizeable concentration of

Shanghainese and was instead surrounded by a sea of locals. But the harder it got, the stronger the yearning. That was why I was still celibate when I was already 31. At the time of applying for admission to the Radio and Television University, the thought of "killing two birds with one stone" had not occurred to me, but after seeing Ye Zi, I suddenly realized opportunity had knocked.

We got married very quickly, and just as quickly we got divorced. I won't go into the details. It's distasteful to badmouth her now that we are divorced. I have never remarried. Of course, it doesn't mean I've had no women all this time. I have a lot of money, a big house, a fine car, social standing, everything. How can I not have women around me? They flock to me. Young, pretty ones, college students, graduate students, you name it. They are eager to befriend me. But I have grown wary of these relationships. I can't help wondering if they are attracted to me as a person or to my wealth. And once that thought enters my mind, it sours the relationship in no time. So the most I could entertain was living together. I could never make up my mind to get married a second time.

Now to pick up where I left off. Last July I was with Xiao Qiong in Dalian. I've been with a dozen women these past years. The relationships ranged widely in terms of intimacy. With some it was mainly dining out together, chatting and going out for fun. I bedded some and lived with a few for varying lengths of time. But it was with Xiao Qiong alone that I truly thought about marriage. She was a reporter from Beijing and we got acquainted after she interviewed me for a story. She was truly a remarkable woman and after half a year together I found I couldn't live without her. We went to Dalian and rented a suite on Bangchui Island. We were inseparable. I'd never had such intense feelings for any other women

I'd been with and the thought of marriage crept into my mind. I thought that since she was twenty years my junior and twenty years older than my daughter, it would not be too awkward for the three of us. We ought to be able to get along. Some men marry a young woman almost their child's age. I always wonder what their children call the new mother.

But I mulled over the thought interiorly without sharing it with her. I've learned one thing in my business career, and that is you can't make an important decision in the heat of the moment. You have to wait until your head cools down and sanity returns before you make the final decision.

I will never forget the week on Bangchui Island. It was the experience of a lifetime. Nothing like it had happened before and nothing like it will ever happen again. The two of us fused into one. We shut out the world; nothing mattered except the two of us being together. That's why I still feel grateful to her even today. At least she allowed me to find out that such a union was possible between a man and a woman. She made it possible for me to experience a happiness not everyone has the good fortune to know.

They say bliss is always followed by a fall. Maybe that's why calamity fell upon us at the height of our ecstasy.

She had left for the beauty parlor that day. I had wanted to accompany her but after several days of deliberately keeping myself unreachable from my company, I decided to stay in our room and make a few phone calls. For days I'd kept my cell phone and beeper switched off, severing all links to the outside world. I did not want our world of two disturbed. In the meantime unbeknownst to us an unthinkable thing was happening that shook the world; the legendary little dragons of Asia had come crashing down almost overnight. I was dealing in timber from Malaysia and had taken out a loan from my bank with all my fixed assets as collateral to pay for the timber. I had done similar deals in the past and had never had a problem. I had no reason to doubt that it would work out this time. If I had known, I would not have come to Dalian. In retrospect though it was a good thing that I had come to Dalian and had cut us off from the world. Had I not, I wouldn't have had such a hauntingly beautiful time with Qiong. Even if I had known about the cataclysm at an earlier stage and had stayed behind at my company headquarters to man the fort, what more could I have done except wait resignedly to be swallowed by the tsunami? One person, one company is so negligible and insignificant in a global financial crisis.

To make a long story short, with economic collapse and currency devaluation, the price of Malaysian timber fell to half of its previous value and the company doing business with me was wiped out. The loan I took out with all my fixed assets as collateral went down the drain. The only prospect before me was to declare bankruptcy and liquidate.

After putting down the phone, I sat alone for two hours in the room until Xiao Qiong came back. In those two hours my head seemed at once crowded with thoughts and yet empty. In fact no amount of thinking was helpful under the circumstances; I had been wiped out. In the wake of my divorce proceedings I had left the house to my ex-wife and had moved into my office. When I had a woman with me for some length of time, as with Xiao Qiong this time, I would stay in a company house. After bankruptcy and liquidation, everything, including real estate and the car, would have to go to the bank. I wouldn't even have a place to stay. I wouldn't even have any private savings because all my money had been invested in the company, except for a few tens of thousands of yuan on my charge card.

Xiao Qiong returned looking splendid and radiant. She did not detect the change in me. I am quite proud of my ability to keep cool in adversity and not show any outward signs of anxiety. Neither high honor nor humiliation can faze me. I consider this the highest virtue of a man. I asked her calmly where she wanted to go for dinner. She suggested Shangri-la. I could understand that. She had just been done up in a beauty parlor, and was eager to show off her beauty and elegance in an equally elegant restaurant. Such occasional bursts of vanity can be quite endearing in a beautiful woman.

We were seated at a table by a full-length window, commanding a panoramic view of the glittering nightscape of Dalian. When we walked into the restaurant, Xiao Qiong attracted a lot of attention. Even I felt a reflected glory. But I knew I would no longer be able to frequent such places in the future, not for a long time at least. I had not made up my mind about when to break the bad news to her, but the moment we walked into Shangri-la I decided I could not put off telling her that I could no longer afford this kind of luxury.

After dinner I ordered coffee for myself and ice cream for her. I added sugar and milk to my coffee and slowly stirred it with a small silver spoon. I asked Xiao Qiong that if I was broke and lost every penny, would she still want to be with me? She looked up from her ice cream and shook her head without hesitation. I asked, what she meant by shaking her head; does it mean she didn't think it was a likely scenario or she will no longer be with me when it happens? She said she meant both. I told her to forget the first part of her answer and tell me if she would still be with me if I became penniless. She again answered without hesitation, no. I felt fine I had nothing to worry about. I told her the truth. She stopped licking her ice cream and stared at me, the questioning look in her eyes turning into one of sheer terror. Then she burst into tears, saying, no, no, it can't be true! I told her to lower her voice as people were turning to look at us. She said amid sobs, to tell her it's not true then. I did not say anything in reply. She bit her lip, the look in her eyes turning into one of despair.

Still stirring my coffee, I explained the situation to her, chapter and verse. She had known about my business in Malaysian timber, so it didn't take a lot of explaining to make her understand what had happened. After that I got to my feet and left the restaurant, leaving the coffee untouched. I didn't really know where I was going. I merely wanted to give her a chance to think it over and we could then go our separate ways.

She followed me out, quickening her pace to catch up with me, and caught my arm. We called a taxi at the door of the restaurant to take us back to Bangchui Island. She was truly a remarkable woman. She acted as if nothing out of the ordinary had happened, as if I had had too much drink. She was solicitous in her care all the way back to our room. When she was undressing me, I said to her, "I'm not drunk." She smiled, saying "I know you're not drunk." That night she was perfect; I can't imagine a more accomplished partner in bed than she was, combining the right measures of tenderness, flirtatiousness, abandon, passion and excitability in her lovemaking. I had thought that I'd be in no mood for sex after the disastrous news, but it turned out to be the best ever night of lovemaking in my life. As I lay spent in bed, too exhausted to move, an expression flashed across my mind: "The Last Supper."

We didn't return to Jiangxi together, having parted in Dalian. The morning after, she said, she'd considered the situation. "The decent thing to do would have been to stick by you in your most difficult moment. But I

know you. You are too proud to want me to
see your sorry state when you are down on
your luck. My presence would only make
you feel worse. But I am confident you will
not stay down for long. You will stand up
again."

I said to her, "Yes, I will seek you out when
I pick myself up." She didn't say anything to
that. I asked, "If I come back for you, will
you still want to come back to me?" She said
she wouldn't. I asked why. She replied, "You
would feel disgusted. What kind of person
would I be in your eyes if I left you when
you fell on hard times and now came back
to you when you'd remade your fortunes?"
In that instant I felt a knife slicing through
my heart, knowing that I was losing her
for good; I was losing an irreplaceable,
wonderful woman. But I had to leave her; it
was dictated by our personalities. We were
destined to walk different paths.

I still miss her very much, even to this
day. When I pick myself up, I will find her

again. I will make an effort even if the odds are ten thousand to one against me … All right, let's change the subject. I always get depressed when I talk about her.

After returning to Nanchang, I made some last ditch efforts, all naturally to no avail. Bankruptcy and liquidation followed. After wrapping things up, I came back to Shanghai because I'd worn out my welcome in Nanchang. Besides, my daughter was in Shanghai, living with my sister. No matter how down and out I was, I couldn't ignore my responsibilities as a father.

Life in Shanghai was tough. I don't blame my sister. I can understand why she acted the way she did. The tables had been turned. Previously I had remitted a monthly allowance of three thousand yuan to my sister for my daughter's upkeep, which obviously cost much less than the stipend. Now I was back in Shanghai and moved in with my sister. I had nowhere to go and couldn't afford to rent a place. My

daughter and I cooked our own meals in my
sister's apartment. We were taken in by my
sister and used her kitchen but were unable
to compensate her in monetary terms, so
we knew better than to do anything to make
our stay any less welcome. In the aftermath
of the cataclysmic change, I felt I'd truly
grown up. I'd mellowed and had come to
terms with my fate. I understood society
invariably respected successful people and
shunned failures like the plague. Only I
didn't want my daughter to be prematurely
exposed to the dark side of human nature
and the unsavory reality of society. She was
still young and should be entitled to her
dreams. So I did not tell her the full story. I
said only that I had tired of being a business
owner with all the pressures and hard work
that came with the position. I had therefore
returned to Shanghai to work for someone
else's company. I didn't tell her I was a
janitor in a hospital and my only request
was for my sister to keep this secret for me.

So now you know why I was suited up in the subway today. I was going to a PTA meeting at my daughter's school.

Four

Several months later the phone rang when I was home, looking for inspiration in front of my computer. I hated it when people called at moments like this but I had no choice but to pick up the phone. You never know who is at the other end, what he or she is going to say to you. Most calls are the most banal and trivial of subjects, but you end up picking it up anyway. You can't cut off all links to the outside world nor would you want to.

An unfamiliar voice said, "This is Lao Wei."

The name did not immediately ring a bell. He detected my embarrassment as I hesitated, but he too seemed embarrassed, at a loss to explain which Lao Wei he was, "I am Lao Wei, you know … from the hospital …"

Now I recognized him. "So you are Lao Wei! How are you?" I was tickled. Didn't he say he'd come to terms with his fate? Why did he still find it so difficult to come out with the word "janitor" when identifying himself? I decided not to mention it. "How have you been?"

"I'm fine. I'd like to invite you to dinner. Are you available?"

"Why don't we do it over the phone? There's no need to go to a restaurant."

After a pause, he said, "Eating in a restaurant is no longer too much of an extravagance for me. If you are available …"

"Oh, so you've remade your fortunes?" I asked.

"No, it's nothing like a big fortune … Can we talk when we meet?"

He knew I'd go. He was too smart not to have detected the strong curiosity gnawing at me.

We met in a small restaurant in my neighborhood. Business was slow and there were not many diners, so it was quiet, ideal for conversation. He was wearing a smart suit. He immediately guessed what I was thinking. "I'm now working for a foreign company and have to follow its dress code."

"Oh, a foreign company! Which one?"

He uttered some English words, but I spoke no English and couldn't tell what company it was, nor was I really interested in finding out. I put another question to him, "What is your position in the company?"

"Assistant to the CEO."

"Not bad at all. How did you get the job?"

"I went through the want ads in the papers and sent out my CV to each and every one of the companies recruiting people. I'd been away for thirty years, so I came back to Shanghai knowing nobody and couldn't get my bearings for a while. I'd lost touch with my high school pals, most of whom would probably not be in positions of power, so I didn't want to bother them. I'd rather rely on myself. Ha! It was all thanks to my inability to be embarrassed. Those who answered the want ads were almost exclusively young people. The better positions went to those with graduate degrees, including PhDs, often earned at prestigious universities. I was clearly the oldest candidate. I practically forced myself on them, saying 'don't be so rigid, how can you successfully run a business when you are so inflexible,' and so on so forth."

I laughed, "I got to hand it to you. Not only are you over age, you don't even possess a competitive degree."

"You are right. All I have is a college degree, earned from the Radio and Television University while working part-time. But let me tell you, paradoxically, this made the companies look at my application with different eyes. I know the way their minds work. They would think that I must have some ace up my sleeve. As the popular saying goes, you wouldn't dare go into the business of mending porcelain ware unless you had a diamond cutter. Why else would someone who does not meet educational and age requirements even bother to apply? He must have some superior skills."

"Then what motivated them to recruit you?"

"I made a persuasive case. I gave them the story of my life, from the days I was a farm worker on a rural production team, to my employment by a government agency, to running a company contracted out to me. I told them how I made a fortune and subsequently tasted financial ruin and ended up working as a janitor in a hospital. I told them everything, chapter and verse, omitting no detail."

"And that persuaded them to hire you?"

"Far from it. Most companies sent me

away with words of comfort. Only two agreed to try me out on a probationary basis. I chose this one. After three months on probation, I was appointed assistant to the CEO. I was full of confidence that if they gave me a chance to prove myself, I would end up with a job. I am indeed superior to the younger recruits, even if they were graduates from prestigious institutions like Tsinghua, Peking or Fudan. If I were a CEO, I would hire someone like me too. First of all such a candidate possesses a wealth of experience, having worked in a government agency, run a business, and has tasted both success and failure. Besides, I went bankrupt not because of my personal failings but as a result of outside forces, something akin to a natural disaster. Secondly, I could endure hardships. I did in the past and still have the same stamina today. No setbacks or difficulties can defeat me. Furthermore my courage in competing against younger people at my age shows my spirit and fortitude. These criteria are much more important than education and age."

I nodded in agreement, "You'll make a comeback. The job at this foreign company will be a way station for you, a chance to catch your breath and regroup. What you need now is to build a network of connections in Shanghai because this is your only Achilles' heel."

Surprisingly he shook his head, "I no longer have the appetite to start a business."

"Why?" I asked. "Is it because it is too tough a challenge, too tiring and the pressure is too much for you?"

"That's not the main reason."

"What's the main reason then?"

"This is why I wanted to see you today. You remember I told you about Xiao Qiong, about Dalian …"

"Oh," I remembered, "have you met again?"

"No," he shook his head, "but I want

badly to see her. After we broke up, I tried to forget her. I thought I could forget her. But I can't for the life of me. A year ago, fresh after bankruptcy, I so badly wanted to remake my fortunes. I have in my character a trait that just won't accept defeat, that wants to succeed despite the odds, if only to prove myself. I had always believed that I was not a man who'd allow himself to be held in thrall to romantic yearnings. But it only showed I may not have really known myself. I did not get romantically entangled before only because I had not yet met a woman that would haunt my dreams, that I could commit myself to. They say that a warrior, no matter how valiant, will shed all defenses when confronted by a beautiful lady. How true that is!"

I laughed.

"Don't laugh. What I mean by a beautiful lady is not a woman blessed with exterior beauty but a fine woman who returns your affection and genuinely cares for you. If you are a true warrior worth his salt, you will be unable to clear this hurdle. It would be easy for a mean-spirited man, on the contrary, to put it out of his mind, because true affection is alien to him."

I stopped laughing, "That is a valid interpretation of the popular saying."

"I wonder, what's a big fortune to me if I don't have Xiao Qiong with me? I need some money to raise my daughter, but not too much. Too much money will only bring grief to my child."

"There's no contradiction between wanting your woman and wanting money."

"But there is a contradiction between wanting Xiao Qiong and wanting money. I told you before, she said 'what would you take me for if I deserted you when you were down on your luck and come back to you when you remade your fortunes?' That means she wouldn't come back to me if I made a fortune."

"But …" I hesitated but decided to say

it anyway, "Excuse my candor, if she'd truly loved you, she would not have left you."

"No, no, you don't understand her," he was anxious to defend her. "She did it for my sake. She knew I had my pride and she was trying to galvanize me into rebuilding my finances."

"And now you've decided against striving toward that goal out of concern that she might not come back to you. Wouldn't that defeat the whole purpose of her noble act?"

"That's why I've come to you for help."

I was baffled, "How can I help?"

"I'd like to ask you to go to her and intercede for me, present my case."

I instantly shook my head, "I doubt it would work. I'm a total stranger to her."

"It will work. Absolutely. A stranger would be more objective. All you need to do is tell her exactly how you got to know me, my present circumstances and my thoughts ..."

"Wouldn't it be better if you went to her directly?"

"… I'm worried that she might not want to see me … If my first overture were rebuffed, I'd have no room for maneuver. It would be better if you could act as some kind of buffer … Of course I hope you'd offer your own thoughts about the whole thing. I think writers are good at empathizing with people. The ability to relate to people's sentiments and feelings is more valuable than anything else. One can give up anything except genuine affection. You can help her analyze the different factors. She and I, together, we can start up a business. With our combined intelligence and strengths, and the catalyst of our mutual affection, there's nothing we can't accomplish."

Seeing my hesitation, he added, "I implore you. She majored in Chinese literature and was a reporter. She has a high regard for writers. You will be that much more effective in making my case."

"Where's she? How do I find her?"

"She's in Beijing. I have her phone number, beeper number and address."

"You want me to go all the way to Beijing to speak to her?"

"The plane tickets and all expenses will of course be on me. You will make a sacrifice in taking time out to do this. But in my view this is also a chance to experience life. This is a gift for a writer like you, isn't it? Our story could become a novel under your pen."

Five

We agreed to meet in the lobby of the Palace Hotel. The venue was picked by Xiao Qiong. Since I said I was not familiar with Beijing, she suggested the Palace Hotel. Obviously she was financially comfortable; I would have chosen a small café.

It was no easy task to find Xiao Qiong. Her phone number, beeper number and address had all changed. I finally got her current beeper number through a friend in the Writers' Association of Beijing, who knew a colleague of hers. But she did not return my call to her beeper. I was on the point of giving up when I remembered that Lao Wei had said she had high regard for writers. So I left my full name, preceded by the words "Writers' Association of Shanghai." That got her to return my call. Truth be told, very few people nowadays show that kind of respect to writers. So my pride got a substantial boost and Xiao Qiong instantly rose in my estimation.

Although the Palace Hotel was populated by beautiful women, I spotted her the moment she walked in. Besides her striking face and figure, she bore herself with a noble elegance. No wonder Lao Wei couldn't forget her.

She began by telling me that she was no longer working for the paper, and that she had created a writing workshop with a few friends.

"What is a writing workshop?" I asked.

She said with a smile, "It is an entity that has emerged to take advantage of a policy loophole. It is, like other businesses, registered with the agency for industry and commerce. It is an independent legal entity but since it is not called a company a large initial investment is not required for registration so there is very little financial risk. As a workshop we contract newspapers, magazines, radio and TV stations to produce programs for them. Under current policy and regulations, private entities are not allowed to publish newspapers, magazines or books, much less own radio or TV stations. What we do is equivalent to producing a magazine of our own except that its articles are scattered among government-run papers and magazines. If and when the government decides to relax its restrictions on media ownership, we can easily reconstitute the articles into a magazine of our own. In our workshop we specialize along the lines of our respective talents and capabilities. Some are into overall planning, some handle computer data, some cover stories in the field and others are responsible for final editing. This makes for high efficiency. We don't normally get paid by the piece but get a percentage from ad revenues."

It all sounded so novel to me and I asked, "Do you also publish books in partnership with publishing houses?"

"Yes."

"How are your earnings?"

"We have just started. We are in the so-called breaking-in stage, so we don't have impressive earnings for the moment, but the prospects are good. It appears you are very interested in our business model."

I nodded, "Yes, I find the idea attractive."

"Are you interested in partnering with us?"

I laughed, "It appears you are like him, the aggressive type."

"Him? Who are you referring to?"

I mentioned Lao Wei's name, watching her closely for any reaction as I said it. She nodded, saying "oh, Lao Wei." She was very calm, exhibiting a sophistication unusual for her age. She abruptly remembered, "Oh yes, what's the purpose of this meeting?"

"Lao Wei asked me to see you."

"Is it about something that concerns him or you?"

"It concerns him."

"Then why is he not here himself?"

I said what Lao Wei expected me to say to her. She listened attentively but offered no comment. Suddenly I had a feeling that I had played a strange, if not outright ludicrous, role in all this. I finally said, "I've accomplished my mission. You may not want to confide in me but you can talk to him directly. Here is his address and phone number."

I stood up to leave but she quickly motioned me to stay, "Wait, wait. Now that you are here, why don't you stay a while longer. I'd like you to send a message to him also."

I sat down. But she relapsed into silence as she drank her coffee in tiny sips spaced far apart. I fished out a cigarette to kill the time and was surprised when she reached out for one too. We took leisurely puffs from our cigarettes. She was sorting out what she was going to say. Apparently it was something hard to convey.

"Why don't you say it to him over the phone. Some things are hard to convey through an intermediary," I said.

"But you already acted as an intermediary."

I sensed displeasure in the tone of her voice. "I know you are already upset, so …"

"I'm not upset. What's there to be upset about? I … I have no wish to speak directly to him, so I'm counting on you. You are already here anyway. You are a writer, so I trust your ability to convey it better than anyone else … I don't want to hurt him. He is a man with ability and character. He's not a bad person. I did find myself intrigued by him while doing an interview with him. I can't say I have no affection at all for him. You may think I was a bit frivolous since you are aware that he and I lived together for a while. Why did I live with him if I didn't feel a strong affection for him? I'm not entirely sure. He's like that too. Many women lived with him without necessarily earning his affection."

I interrupted her, "But he does have affection for you and believes it is mutual."

"I'm really sorry, but I never thought he'd take it seriously, because I knew he'd had many women and I was just one of the many. I thought we just enjoyed making love and affection didn't much come into the equation."

"The day you left each other, he was greatly touched by the way you behaved toward him. That probably led him to believe that you must also …"

She asked, looking at me, "What was I supposed to do under the circumstances? In one day he fell from the top of the world into hell. Could I have immediately left him? To put it crudely, given the amount of money I'd received from him over time, some kind of professional ethic was called for on my part."

I was struck speechless, feeling devastated for Lao Wei.

She flashed a faint smile, "I said I was sorry. But actually he has no real cause to feel wronged. Many women were treated as shabbily by him. I am not trying to avenge those women, but objectively we are even now."

I nodded. What could I say to that?

Six

I did not tell Lao Wei what really happened, saying merely that I had not succeeded in finding Xiao Qiong. She had changed jobs, her address, phone and beeper number, so it was only natural that I had been unable to locate her. Lao Wei was deeply disappointed but there was nothing to be done.

I returned to my daily routine. My days were full and soon Lao Wei began to fade from my memory. Come autumn I attended an opening ceremony for a book fair. Not having had a chance to browse the bookstores for quite a long time, I drifted from one exhibition hall to another, very much like a famished traveler invited to a feast, unable to pull himself away. Although my bookshelves were already stuffed full, I couldn't resist the temptation of books that struck my fancy. I bought one after another, and pretty soon they added up and by the time I left I had a big bagful of them. I waited for a taxi by the curbside. On most days I'd find plenty of vacant cabs but for some reason all the taxis that whizzed by were occupied. Maybe it was the overcast sky foreshadowing rain that prompted more people to take taxis. I walked on, lugging the heavy bag of books, all the while keeping an eye on taxis cruising in the street. Suddenly a motorcycle screeched to a halt at my side, startling me. I stared angrily at the motorcyclist, signaling strong disapproval, only to see a smile greet me. It was a familiar smile too. When the helmet was removed, I recognized Lao Wei.

Lao Wei the biker was no longer wearing a suit but dressed like a cowboy. He gave the impression that he was on the road a lot. "Are you heading home?" he asked.

I nodded.

"I'll give you a ride." Without waiting for a reply, he grabbed the heavy bag of books and put it in the toolbox of the bike. I thankfully got on the back seat and the machine shot forward like a bullet.

This being my first time on a motorcycle, my heart instantly rose to my throat. He was driving too fast, too recklessly, weaving in and out of motor vehicles of all shapes and sizes. All I could do was stare ahead and leave my life, or death, in the hands of God and Lao Wei. I could breath normally again only when the bike came to a stop by the curb.

He did not take me to my home. It was only then that I remembered he never knew where I lived. When I was about to tell him my address, he invited me for a beer.

We went to a rather unique beer house where the tables stretched from the interior all the way to the walls of the central atrium. The tables and chairs were made of rattan and the floor was paved with slate. The casualness of the rustic décor showed a conscious design. Lao Wei was on familiar terms with the owner of the beer house. He was clearly a regular patron.

The owner asked, "What kind of beer would you like?"

Lao Wei asked me.

"Any beer."

"They carry dozens of brands, make your pick," he handed the drink menu to me.
"I'm no connoisseur, anything light will be fine for me."

He told the owner, "Four bottles of the Canadian beer I had last time."

After the owner left our table, I said, "It seems you are living a good life."

He shook his head, "Not exactly a good life. I'm just trying to get as much as possible out of life, trying to be good to myself."

"What have you been doing?"

"I've started a business offering express delivery services."

"Oh, an express delivery company."

"No, not an express delivery company in the usual sense," he corrected me. "It is an express delivery services company."

"What is an express delivery services company?"

He explained, "We offer many more services than merely the physical delivery of goods. We act as agents for purchasing, payments and all kinds of application filing. In life you inevitably need to deal with bureaucracies of one kind or another. It is costly, time-consuming and involves a lot of hurdles for people unfamiliar with the processes and the workings of the organizations one has to deal with. Sometimes when you finally get the hang of it, you will no longer have to go through the same process again. For us professionals such hurdles are less of a problem."

I nodded in agreement.

He continued, "In my vision of the future, everyone will have three advisers, one family doctor as health adviser, one lawyer as legal adviser and an agent like my company to deal with the tedious transactions of life. Doctors and lawyers need to have a college education and professional certificates, so not everyone can become one. Service agents like us are an emerging profession that the government hasn't come around to regulating yet."

"How many employees do you have in the company?"

"The express delivery services company employs about sixty. All of them are laid-off workers. It is actually a subsidiary of the service agency I referred to a while ago. I started this subsidiary because it didn't require a hefty initial investment. All we needed was a phone, a beeper and a modest means of transportation, a motorcycle, usually a hybrid one."

"And you are the CEO of the subsidiary?"

He nodded.

"You've decided to become a CEO after all … because you have been unable to find Xiao Qiong?"

"Not entirely. I did not expect I'd become a CEO. I was still working for the foreign company. Once I casually mentioned the idea of a service agency to my boss. The concept was nonexistent in his country because they already had a well-developed service industry so getting things done is not as cumbersome as here. Usually a lawyer would suffice. Starting a business in China has taught him how complicated it is to have to deal with so much bureaucracy. He liked my idea very much and insisted that I be in charge of this new business. He didn't want to give it to a younger person, who'd lack the kind of social experience and exposure that I possess."

"Your boss was right."

"He offered me the position of CEO, shares and a seat on the board. It was an offer I couldn't refuse."

"It appears you are doing quite well."

"I can't complain. I think I'm doing okay."

He glanced at me, laughed self-deprecatingly and lowered his head to finish his beer in slow sips. Then he let out a soft sigh, "You know it's not like that, not like that ... I would approve of myself, feel great about myself if I were younger, but at my age I know I am nothing."

"Don't say that. You're doing well. Not many men can drive as hard as you to achieve the heights of success and come to terms with humiliating defeat with as much grace and resilience."

He said with a shake of his head, "That's just the exterior."

He filled his glass and took a large gulp of beer, almost emptying half of the glass. I suddenly thought of Xiao Qiong; did they meet after my Beijing trip? A man as clever as he couldn't have been easily duped by my lies.

"Did you manage to find her; did you try to find her again?"

He interrupted me, "Let's not talk about her. Let's not talk about her. Let's drink! Boss, four more bottles."

I didn't press the subject. We drank bottle after bottle, at a leisurely pace, until he finally succeeded in getting himself drunk.

Seven

I've never seen Lao Wei again after that, but for unexplainable reasons he comes into my thoughts a lot, so does Xiao Qiong. I have a nagging feeling that what Xiao Qiong said to me in Beijing did not come from her heart. They were truly made for each other; they were so compatible, birds of a feather as it were. If they had worked together, they'd have achieved faster and greater success. Maybe they have met again and have formed a collaborative relationship and have succeeded. I'm on constant watch, looking forward to the day when I'll see news coverage in the papers and on TV about his services agency and when his company's ads will be splashed across town.

I can't explain why I look forward to it, but
I do earnestly hope for the day.

Stories by Contemporary Writers from Shanghai